THE MYSTERY OF LOVE

THE MYSTERY OF LOVE

ANDREW MEEHAN

An Apollo Book

This is an Apollo book, first published in the UK in 2020 by Head of Zeus Ltd
This paperback edition first published in 2021 by Head of Zeus Ltd

9 7 5 3 1 2 4 6 8

A catalogue record for this book is available from
the British Library.

ISBN (PB): 9781789544909
ISBN (E): 9781789544879

Typeset by Divaddict Publishing Solutions Ltd

Printed and bound in Great Britain by
CPI Group (UK) Ltd, Croydon CR0 4YY

Head of Zeus Ltd
First Floor East
5–8 Hardwick Street
London EC1R 4RG

WWW.HEADOFZEUS.COM

For Elizabeth and George Meehan

“The mystery of love is greater than the mystery of death.”

Oscar Wilde

Contents

Could You Direct Me to the Crocodile Enclosure?

i

It is for recreation & nothing more that she has cut up all those oranges. The little one in particular is being very greedy. Woe betide anyone getting between him & his breakfast. But that much fruit is enough to give an infantryman the runs for a week.*

The JOYS OF PARENTHOOD, she is all too aware of those, with a certain someone forever at pains to point them out. One thing he has never mentioned, because it would never occur to him to, is the great amount of time absorbed by the little animals. Constance cares for them as best she can but they demand entertainment around the clock, & entertain them she must.

She remembers many years ago their father, a certain someone, making himself a mouth of teeth from the peel of his breakfast grapefruit.

Could you direct me to the crocodile enclosure? he said.

---

* Have all you want, boy.

She laughed so hard that she almost swallowed her spoon.

She tries it now.

Could you direct me to the crocodile enclosure?

Secretly, she hasn't much interest in playing games, if she ever had. Secretly, she is not always interested in her children, especially when they're being so skittish. The little one won't sit still for more than one moment & when she attempts to manoeuvre some peel into the older one's mouth he turns his face away then tosses the peel onto the bloody floor.

Wasn't this supposed to be fun?

Relief comes in the form of a shadow across the table. Mister Sconomiglio appears in the doorway before skimming a couple of letters across the tiles.

The postman likes to remind her that the last people got mail once a week at the most. Did they have the misfortune to have an estranged husband who would, through force of habit, have plenty that is fragrant to say to the likes of a postman? But he is not here, is he? Not that you would know it, with the sight of another letter with the Reading postmark. Only then does she remember her orange-peel teeth, removing them to call out to the postman as he departs.

Lovely to see you too, Mister Sconomiglio. I expect we'll see you again at the same time tomorrow.

The poor man won't understand her & she doesn't care anyway.

The little one has been tearing the stamps from the envelopes, discarding the letters so that, helped along by all the peelings, there is the makings of a hearty bonfire.

Don't, darling. They're not your property.

The little one makes his way under the table & lies there like a bag of washing—one day he'll crawl through the floorboards & be gone—only to emerge with an interest in what's outside in the orange grove, which can mean only one thing.

It's about time they were ready for school. & what's their worry? Times tables are times tables.

& she'll read the letter on the way to the doctor's. The backache whips up at the very thought of the trip into Genoa. It comes from inside of her, often with a power that can overwhelm. Sometimes she thinks the pain is connected to the end of her marriage, & that it's a sustaining pain. This is very much not what you share with a doctor, least of all an Italian who is more inclined to dispense lozenges as a cure. Why can't the doctors give her something with a name? TB—a good case of it, dreadful but survivable. That would suit her down to the ground; she could go on to say how much she has suffered.

She keeps a small block of wood to hand, for the quags when they come make her want to bite down on something hard. Is that why the little one has taken to biting the older one whenever there's a dispute? & disputes tend to arise thirty or forty times an hour, over soup spoons or the existence of fairies.

& when she thinks it over it's quite apparent that in certain circumstances she is herself a biter.

Stand up for yourself, quite right.

*

What does she love more, Italy or parenting? On a day like today, there is one clear victor.

This house—& the garden, in all its colours—has provided what she asked of it & more; the days feel shorter but also open-ended. Even taking into account the mess it has made of her table, she will never tire of fruit hanging from trees. Each morning as she dresses she feels a sense of release. The sound her bare feet make against marble. & this blouse, it wouldn't do to go about like that in London. You'd be as well to stroll down Pall Mall in your nightie.

Marriage is a sacrament. & even as she hoped hers would last forever, of course she never believed it would last the day. It was for some reason the biggest decision she would ever make & she did it with the same forethought as you would use to pick out a spool of thread.

She would like to be in love, with someone, anyone, something. Lovely love, frictionless & sudden & yielding. & can't you be drawn to love without it having to be everlasting? For abstinence is just as exhilarating as intimacy. She has become aware of the slightest changes in air pressure. The air seems to be where it begins, the need for it, the sex they aren't having—she isn't having. Once she can survive those urges, she can worry less & not resent their intrusion, for what use are urges to her?* That THE BREATH OF LOVE hasn't drifted off entirely but has transformed itself into a consoling form of

* Have I just walked in on you? For it's less & less that I know of you. It is as if by witnessing this scene, I have yet to put you through a thing.

hard-heartedness is a source of great relief & only occasional regret.

Let's see what this governess makes of you today, shall we? Where are those uniforms?

The children have had to be re-attired from scratch. The workmanship being of a reasonable standard, it must be said, although given where they are in the world the fabrics are considerably lighter. Loose cotton is all very well for her, but flimsiness is not what the boys are used to—& the bigger one, who is as raw & skinny as a sapling, has noticed that all too well.

Mama? When can we wear our own clothes?

Those are your clothes, dearest.

I feel silly.

A silly billy?

Just silly.

I happen to like them.

She wonders if the bigger one's uncertainty, over his clothing & much else, derives at least in part from an expectation of a visit from his father—which is unlikely to happen, isn't it?*

& yet still she expects OW to stroll in as if nothing has happened, closing the shutters against THE BEST OF THE DAY & in the same gesture reassuring her that she has coped rather well in the unusual circumstances of his

* It's true that I was enfeebled by one, & to the other's charm I was simply immune.

absence & that everything can go back to an approximation of the way it was, not before passing comment on the boys' uniforms & the bareness of the shutters & the dismal furnishings, only to be told that all of that now is none of his business.

ii

One hundred & eleven steps—all well & good on the way down to the village. All very virtuous on the way up. The way up can be considered later.

Now is the time to enjoy the sweetness of the air & what flashes of sea are visible through the fig branches. There is so much sky, only a beast or a stone would not be overwhelmed by it. On both sides of the staircase is an assortment of fruit trees, including one whose branches remain frustratingly out of reach for the little one.

Arancione. Oranje. Oranssi. Narancs. Laranja.

He jumps on each word.* Another wild swipe whereupon a fruit falls & hits him on the head before tumbling down the steps towards Constance. She kicks it farther down the steps towards the bigger one, waiting as ever for his brother to do whatever it is he does every morning.

ArancioneOranjeOranssiNarancsLaranja.

---

* It's so lovely to picture a small boy leaping. I've seen Vyvyan be as fascinated with a dead bird. As a boy I gather I was an awful one for a muddy puddle.

Constance can hardly decipher him.

Your governess will be delighted to meet such a young linguist, she says.

That was Italian then Dutch, Finnish, Hungarian & Portuguese, which is similar to Spanish.

That'll do.

Although, given their place on the globe, not as close as you might think

May I remind you, darling, that you are nine years old? & you should not see it as your imperative to always have the last word.

The little one begins to follow her down the steps. Constance is pleased for once at his obedience. For there is more than a whisper of his father about him.

No, Mama. Of course not.

The children sit at minuscule desks before a nervous young governess. Signora Belotti herself is the size of a child, a small child choked by a corset.

Does it matter that this young woman has a squint? Will that make her unobservant, & will it mean the children won't take her seriously? Does it matter that the children do not have the correct footwear for school? It matters in the way that their happiness matters, which is to say NOT AT ALL.*

* Important—nay, essential—to regard them as puppets, innocuous finger puppets that could be returned to their box at the end of a trying day. & what if on the occasional morning one forgot to remove them from their box?

Constance will have a look for new shoes when she gets to Genoa, whenever she gets there. But the little one won't let go of her skirts.

Signora Belotti goes around the room, asking the children to say their names.

Come ti chiami?

One by one the children answer.

Mi chiamo Giorgio Cravero.

Mi chiamo Lucia Conterno.

There's a little American girl called Sylvia Paterson & a nervous Russian boy finds himself helped along by the bigger one.

Il suo nome è Vladimir.

The little one yawns to show that he is not one bit impressed by his brother. Nor, it is to be said, is his mother. She does not after all these years understand WHAT MAKES THE BOY TICK. He really is a bit of a pain.

But the bigger one continues.

Mi chiamo Cyril Holland.

Molto bene, Cyril, says the governess, pronouncing his C as if his name is cheer or chariot.

The little one detaches himself from his mother. It was always only a matter of time before he decided the classroom was there for the conquering.

Mi chiamo Vyvyan Wilde, he says.

Certainly he has inherited more than a name from his father.

Holland, darling.

Il tuo nome è Vyvyan Holland, the governess says.

Her son regards his teacher as though he is facing a firing squad & she is its leader.

With speech slow & deliberate, he says, Mi chiamo Vyvyan Wilde.

iii

The sights to be seen on an Italian train. Cats & chickens & every second compartment hosting a family picnic. Chatter chatter chatter. The people are not one bit restrained. How she has tried, but no amount of gesticulating has ever made her understood to anyone around here.

It's as if she has been transported to the morgue. A barefoot gentleman is sprawled asleep in the seat across from her. She wants to POKE HIM to make sure he's alive. The very sight of a man's monstrous feet makes Constance so agitated that she begins to make her way along the carriage to look for an empty compartment.

A train compartment, perfectly stuffy, is not quite the place in which to suffer a crisis. But she is just in the mood for one. For there's one of the little one's oranges in her pocket, & an orange fresh from the tree is too fresh. The juice is livid. & what she'd like now is not an orange but a nice apple, a nice English apple, stored for the winter before being cut into quarters & put on a nice china plate. Cut into quarters & put on a plate & thrown at the wall.

She takes a seat by a window at the very moment the train crosses a rugged gorge. The sense of a drop, & a vision of someone falling from the train to their death, reminds her that the first letter of the morning was, of course, from OW. Diligent about his work as never before. & filled with profuse, blaring APOLOGIES, as his letters always are.

Yes, darling, all this *is* your fault.

No, I don't suppose you are cut out for hard labour. Now, what else would you like to say?*

There is a solitary cloud in the sky. Constance feels it following her.

The second letter is fixed with a seal, the light falling on the wax she takes great enjoyment in tearing apart. Her gaze skims the legalese, alighting on the phrase:

> Please note that by deed poll dated February 20th 1896 I renounced the name Constance Wilde & assumed the name Constance Holland.

She returns the letter to its envelope & feeling unexpectedly & SHAMEFULLY PROUD tucks it under her.

Genoa is not far off now.

& is it so reprehensible to love your own name?

Ever since their father's business, the boys have been too concerned with who they are. Their farewell to England

* I bloody well built the boys a rabbit hutch, don't you remember?

was made as if they were being hauled from a lovely dream. They sit around & talk about home, & it is all far too much. For Tite Street was not their home but hers & Oscar's.

That house lies empty, but they can visit if they want to. & aren't there thousands of places they could live? She is quick to tell the boys that they don't like London anyway & that no one does.

iv

She walks along an empty alleyway, soaked in slum-darkness. In the courtyard before Doctor Bossi's rooms, there are children, quite a few, playing in their underclothes. Her eyes widen for a glimpse of a parent.

A woman of too great an age to be left in charge of anything living &/or valuable watches from a doorway. Under her headscarf, her hair is a right bird's nest. She is—a first in this country—completely silent, & is praying. Would that she be praying for everyone here.

Next door is a restaurant overseen by the overly gracious waiter in a jacket that is not quite white, it is white like bread.

Sometime between this world & the next, she sees herself dining there, with Oscar selecting their fish from the glass case—there is very little he won't do for a good meal. But she imagines him grumbling about the waiter, the colour of his jacket & that he is being shy with the wine.* But there is nothing much she can do about that today.

More steps, & five flights of PURE GLOOM. Constance enters his rooms, knowing to let herself in & that since Bossi has no help she will have to announce herself too.

Bossi is reading. As far as she knows, he never leaves the fifth floor.

He is a heavy little man who walks with a crutch, not a very encouraging sign in a physician. His shoes are dusty, the room is dusty, & the clock isn't keeping time.

He doesn't look up, sulking—no doubt—before they have even begun. Constance, with her tongue held tight, stands before him & starts to undress. THAT GETS HIS ATTENTION. She feels the man's eyes on her. It has been a while since she has had anyone's eyes on her.

How to consider your call on another's desire without imagining its absence? Wasn't it the pursuit of something that wasn't there? If you sought satisfaction, you craved disappointment. That was the bargain.

But the poor man is sick & SO IS SHE.

Bossi must be able to see that she is watching him, & yes he pretends that he is staring into space. Any minute now, to prove the point, he'll start picking his nose.

There he goes! There he goes! Eating it.

Yesterday she promised the little one a few bob if he'd stop doing the same at the dinner table & he signed up to the deal.

---

* How very lonely it was for you to eat alone.

But later in bed she caught him doing it, which was an affront to the child, as the bed was his own domain, he said, & there he should be allowed to do as he pleased.

What is the doctor's excuse? He has the look of a man who WOULDN'T CARE if half the world saw him wiping his bottom in the street. Publically wiping your bottom is probably the kind of thing that passes for a conversation-starter around here.

She doesn't like the man & nor is she satisfied with his diagnosis, what there is of it.

A chilly expression & a smile that displays his teeth—corroded stumps—& no amusement. Already she feels as though SHE HAS WASTED A TRAIN JOURNEY.

When she is encouraged to go behind a screen & get down to her corset, she sees his breakfast things are still sitting out.

Through the canvas he says, Mrs Wilde, if I may? Young children are all the exercise a woman needs.

One could almost say he is reading from a transcript of their previous conversations.

Holland, Constance says.

& the examination, much like all the others, is a charade. As if this is a showing of ponies, she is invited to walk up & down the room. Foolishly she obeys when he asks her to go to the window & to turn her face towards the light.

The building is rotting. A dead bird on the sill—she has enough proprietary feelings to want to take it home. Where is her camera now? For SOME REASON, destitution is a source of perpetual fascination—to pull up a chair by the window &

wait for winter. Once the bird has putrefied it will freeze solid. May God spare it.

The children can be heard playing outside. There is an ongoing dispute.

What you may like to call creeping paralysis is grandiose language for back strain, Bossi says.

She hesitates before saying, & you, doctor? You seem rather listless yourself. Have you—?

Nothing sea air & exercise won't fix.

In doctors' rooms, as at home or anywhere, Constance has no wish to be spoken over, especially by someone with the defeated note one only hears in the elderly & the indolent. She is patient in many ways but has been impatient, too, of a brother & a mother & an aunt &, even worse, a husband who have seen it as their position to speak for her & over her.

She might sometime soon stop talking altogether. This mute version of herself is very appealing. She will pick a day to do it.

Bossi begins waving his hands around the small of her back without going near her.* He claps his hands.

Time.

Once outside in the light of day she feels immediately well.

---

* Touch her, man, go on.

v

There's a warm breeze coming in through the train window. That & a placid sea allow her to be unequivocal about the decision to leave England. Quite how she ever survived the winters, she doesn't now understand. So much easier to live quietly in a foreign place where she knows hardly anyone & perhaps will never get to know anyone. It makes her more relaxed, in a way, for there to be no sense that anyone is looking at her & might have an opinion of whether she is suffering from scarlet fever or a sore bum.

Home late enough for Francesca to have given the boys their dinner. Constance hears that in her absence they have embarked upon a life of eating with proper cutlery. But the boys—at least the bigger one—have been asking questions.

She is convinced they are better off out of England & away from it all. She can see it in their bronzed skin & in their faces. Little boys should not have a care in the world.* Oh, for the day when they'll be old enough to play patience & make themselves useful with the spring clean.

In the evenings the sun imprints itself on the drawing room floor, a chequered pattern of light wherein the little one lies roasting. He'd preen himself until morning if he was let, using his brother as a pillow. They have wonderful shapes, the little animals.

* Their bodies, our spirits. So solemn were they for ones so young. In some cultures, children never grow old.

The little one is perfectly happy to torment his brother, for which there'll be no consequences.

Constance goes to her bedroom to change into Arabian trousers & a loose shirt. She takes the Kodak from the table & stands the boys up at the windows.

I'm sure Papa would like to see a photograph of you both.

She gets on with the picture, thinking, Am I seeing them as they are? A little boy's soul, what is it but a will-o'-the-wisp?

The custom of portraiture calls for composure enough to arrest the moment. To allow itself to be read, the soul must keep still. You are as well, are you not, trying to pocket a young faun?

Turn the key, pull the string, done! the little one says with a yell.

& it has to be said that pictures don't take as much deciphering as people do. But she does not want the boys to get used to being looked at. No need for them to become prey like their father.

Come, she says, moving them around to catch the light. Small before tall. I shall send the prints to Papa.

The little one, immaculate in boredom, insists on posing alone in the fading light. She takes his photograph, at which he deflates as if exhausted from all the effort of doing very little.

Mi chiamo Vyvyan Wilde.

You'll get used to it, darling.

She takes him into her lap. He is too much for the eye. Better by far to keep him protected.

vi

For hours now she has lain on the ground. The small, lively boats in the bay. The sea above & sky below. But no sign today of the light of God. At least the lying about has broken the back of the morning.

She has never been so happy. She has never been so bored. It's all everyone else's fault. Not quite the children's fault, but they're under her feet all the same so blame them she might. The thought of blaming anyone but Oscar for her boredom repulses her. & it amuses her. The worst of both. Between boredom & amusement there can be no winner. & one thing she is sure of: she is so rested as to be almost incapable of pressing a button.

But Constance is hell-bent on mastering this camera contraption. She has it almost figured out but not quite.

A damned cry then as Francesca rushes into the grove. She is shaking & has about her the usual helpless air. But there is no way for Constance to blame anyone else for her own wasted morning.

For reasons unknown the children remained indoors before school—they wouldn't be convinced that the constancy of the sun brings with it a responsibility to be out in it.

The bigger one will spend unhurried hours at the kitchen table, drawing or not, with only the occasional spat with his brother. He is the better draughtsman, but it's another matter that the little one is by far the more expressive.

Signora Hollanda? Francesca says.

English, if you please.

Francesca has for the children's sake been rather too dogged about hanging on to her Italian. There is a breed of local woman who sees no life beyond their own village walls. This one came with the house & they are stuck with her now. But, having nothing else to do with herself, she works from morning till night.

Madame Holland.

Do go on.

A man whom be in the kitchen.

Well, well, well, Constance says, making her way as slowly as she can through the trees, her heart beating in her brain. Nothing at all under her feet but memories of love. Absorbed light, more colour, more. One day, when they have all been buried in ground as rich as this, she will be reborn in a scatter of seeds. But what use is a seed that doesn't sprout?

& trust Oscar to appear when she isn't ready. Only he would excuse that.

Constance is harassed by too many tender thoughts. Once, when he was supposed to have been in Worthing with one of his little friends, Oscar turned up at Tite Street to surprise them. There was some to-do about biscuits for the children. She—& they—could barely speak from all the excitement. Only to them, his family, did Oscar ever reveal this side of himself.

Nor has he written in a while, so she positively knew something was up.

It's not that the correspondence won't be missed. She has been getting sick of all the sorrys as well as bored of being angry, the purpose of which has been lost to the fever haze of the Ligurian Sea.

They will after today have no more of all that.

What will they *do* here? None of this has been prepared for. As long as Oscar makes himself useful. She will tell him so.

At this very moment it is preferable to be a beast or a stone. A beast that could weep. A stone that could sing a cheerful song.*

Another moment or two will be necessary to pull herself together. She lets Francesca go on.

Tell him I'll be there in a minute. & see to the spare bedroom, will you?

The windows in the downstairs bedroom work as a mirror, in the way you'd see at a funhouse. That uses up all of two seconds.

In all this she has forgotten about her appearance. Most of the time she will pass a mirror without noticing herself. Empty skies, empty days. But the windows do offer a gleam that she has been lacking. Nor are Oscar's letters any replacement for the real thing. Their shared past is something to be proud of & it is nothing to be proud of. But his frailty was… understandable is a good word for it.

---

* It wasn't always that your train of thought took as much following as my own. Isn't there another feeling attributable to this moment? Can't you name it, no?

Oscar was silly & cruel, & more than once.* When he was being mean he behaved like some people did when they were trying to make a favourable impression: gentle, & persistently inquisitive. This cruelty was not God given—the acts were all his own. & this is all she has ever cared to say aloud on the matter.

Any thought she has given to his incarceration has been too much. Nay, Constance has thought of him too much & to no end. The feeling invoked by this unexpected visit is an affront to her thinking soul. She alternates, loyal & not—a magnet, with a magnet's failings.

Failing to imagine the life of another as her own. For too long Constance has been able to tolerate anything she can't see. & let us all wipe away the sheen that time & time again coats the loyal woman. There is no such thing. Nor is there any one thing that counts as love. There are only separate & different loves. & for the acceptance of this as a matter of fact she has Oscar to thank. Had she been coming to see them as brother & sister? Such is a marriage, yet her love will always be that of a wife. & her felt truths are those of a mother.

vii

Oh, it's you, she says in her smallest voice.

The day is suddenly less spacious than it was.

* What is it that makes you think I can't hear?

The fellow's outfit cannot pass unnoticed. There are not too many who suit the parchment-stiff linens of the Anglo abroad. She would compare Robbie to a little boy in fancy dress, except to say that there has been something of a ripening, he is quite a bit stouter than of yore.

No 'quite' & no 'something' about it either.

You're not to worry, Constance dear. Everything is the same with Oscar. More's the pity.*

A much firmer hand shall have to be kept on her expectations. & it counts as strange that someone came all the way from England to confirm that all is as it was.

You've been busy, Robbie says, standing a little too late to greet her.

Or words to that effect.

He has brought nothing with him. If Robbie thinks she cannot see that he is here to snoop he is damnably mistaken. He has helped himself to some orange juice, she sees. What if it poisoned him?

With no great eagerness, Constance says, Do eat all the oranges you can. I dare say they are hard to come by in England.

England has a lot to answer for; that is quite certain.

Robbie, are you sure everything is all right?

Given Oscar's whereabouts, he's what you might call beleaguered.

---

* So this is where Robbie was off to. I understand, perfectly. But it's not this at all that I'm listening for.

We could be here all day talking about the ghastliness of life in prison.

Whatever it is Robbie is up to, he's floundering already. Constance is about to settle at the table when she is startled by the sight of the name-change certificate sitting proudly. It's nobody's business what she is & isn't called, but only a fool would telegraph such news to the world. This optimism over a new name isn't very much, is it? But it shall remain all hers for the time being.

Quickly, on top of the certificate she places Oscar's letters. There are enough of them to make a nice book.

He has been corresponding I see, says Robbie.

Poor devil. I don't know what to say to him.

What has he had to say for himself?

What do you have to say for *yourself*?

By this circumspection she is becoming guarded. The dance she has found herself in, & Robbie's two left feet, would take the life out of you.

My visit owes itself to pressures brought to bear on us all by the bankruptcy based on Oscar's conviction. In the event of a divorce—

In the event of? I have yet to make up my mind either way. What do you have to say to that?

That Oscar would have to turn to his friends. Not all of whom are as reliable as I am.

Allow me to say that it's not like you to be so tiresome.

She could be more polite. She should be more polite. But she would have gambled on the fact of Robbie being here on some gutless crusade. THE NICETIES were only going to last so long.

& that she has assumed a stance at the window Robbie should take for a warning. She might be advised to report to him of warships in the distance. It would not only be comical but appropriate if there were.*

Should you permit, he says, I would ask how you would feel about agreeing to an annuity?

My feelings wouldn't come into it. & I don't have as much time as you may think for idle conversation. Do bear in mind that it is Oscar who has transgressed. You expect me to join him in captivity?

The morning has burned off into another pleasant afternoon. But her afternoon heart is a solemn one &, if she were alone at this point in the day, she would be succumbing to a lie-down. Some afternoons when it is time to fetch the children from school she feels as though she is being raised from her deathbed.

She can feel now the presence of someone coming headlong up the stairs. Could today be the day Mister Sconomiglio appears to them in sprightly form? Evidently not. There is nothing approaching a knock on the door. Not even a tap. & she has today very little time either for her husband's lovers or for tormented postmen.

Mister Sconomiglio, perhaps feeling the righteous burn

* Would that have been all-out war, or all-out surrender? This was the ultimate question, to which I have never been able to provide an answer.

of her gaze, places the mail on the table. A retreat is made without a murmur.

My, Oscar is persistent, Robbie says.

Not a hint as to what it may contain, but the envelope does not feature Oscar's handwriting. Nor does it bear a familiar postmark.

Inviting Robbie to step away from her, she opens the letter.

AGAIN & AGAIN she reads it & in that way she cannot resist pictures a life lessening; skies emptying & a tree with its branches bare. A body falling weightlessly towards heaven. No one escapes it, the going brown & so on. Safest to call it relief to hear from Mister Death, for there is also a touch of revenge about it. An obscenity that is very soothing to Constance as she considers all there is to be to done.

It will be a mercy if she can find someone to break the news. She will not be so self-serving as to do it herself. Even if it's not going to be her, someone will have to do it. He will need putting out of his misery. If only there were a way in which he could be given the news without actually having to be told it.

The sunlit room grows by degrees chilly & dark as she says, Poor Oscar.

I Only Want to Dress Up as Me

i

The grand republic of Piccadilly. Long & straight for good reason. Horses at the whip could proceed as if in Alexandra Park.

But her driver had for a good reason been asked to go as slowly as he could. & did he KNOW where he was going? The way here was supposed to be a simple loop around the park. With so much building going on, it was impossible to know where you were these days. That was London for you, a debauch. Everyone was from somewhere else, the people as bewildered as the horses. The increase in the population was, according to Otho, becoming unsustainable.

& if her dear brother said it, it had to be true. Otho was also of a mind that going to hear OW was akin to being in the presence of a rather louche preacher.

Was she not, in the spirit of inquisitiveness, on her way to worship? Her mind was on anything but reverence. Let it NOT BE like being at church. OW would have to be the liveliest & most persuasive of orators for this not to be like church. She thought she might one day preach to him. For she knew a thing or two about beauty. Every second thought she had was on the matter. Might she tease him with hers?

Where to now, miss? said the driver.

He had been talking all along & she hadn't been able to make out a word. She hadn't made the effort.

NOWHERE, was the answer.

Nor was it a woman's job, by the way, to know where they were going. Was it not their job to sit up straight & whisper? It was for ANOTHER REASON ENTIRELY that Constance had not been speaking freely nor breathing easily. Only this morning something of a stand had been made. Even though she had for aeons been saying as much, both to Dolly & to Aunt Emily, it was not without a struggle that a goodbye was said to her corset.

Let's not, they all said.

But her very liver & lungs were being squeezed out of it. At the end of any day her ribs would be livid & criss-crossed from their entrapment. So no more, she said, of the straps & lacing & all that cruel geometry marked on her skin.* Aunt Emily was not the only one to have strong views on corsets & their benefits. But Constance carried herself perfectly well & her posture was not in need of correction.

Hadn't she the audacity to believe there was more to a woman's appeal than an extenuated waist? She wasn't about

* I'll have you know there are people in the world who enjoy being choked.

to debase herself to get one. Hers was a woman's body not a man's, she needed no reminding. There was no need to exaggerate the fact.

They had been working their way along so slowly—& now they were going so fast. A bump in the road, well timed, would have done for the carriage & her both. She needed to collect herself, try at the very least. The feeling in her ribs had moved—where? Down, perhaps. It was there somewhere, quivering.

& when they arrived she didn't want to go into the hall. She wanted to stay where she was, relaxing in the carriage as though she were at home—well, she wasn't.

She arranged herself, directing her best & most condescending smile to the back of the driver's neck. What was it—soot?—on the man's collars? Most likely it was. Here was the value of the hackney's seating configuration. It was the driver who had to swivel around in order to speak. One could sit tight until it was time to step outside. But it was not time yet.

She tried to think of a reason why. Arriving late was ONE WAY to be noticed, & being noticed was likely cause for Constance to pass out. A fellow latecomer might catch her eye, & the avoidance of eye contact was as much of an undertaking as being looked at.

People more often than not were friendly—& how could you not like friendly?—but when A PERSON would ask you, for instance, what time you got some place, they really meant to ask when would you be leaving. That was why she didn't like small talk; she wasn't interested in asking questions about people's lives.

Where to?

If he said that again, she'd be sharpening her tongue. & if she was going to get herself worked up today it was not to be over a cab man.

Just to make it seem as though she had rushed, & as though she had had something to do, Constance trotted the last few steps to the door of the hall. She was happy to live with those kinds of lies.

A voice came from within, the one she had been waiting to hear. & what did it matter that the immediate reaction was to feel muddled? But this happened often. & in the delivery there was a tone she recognised, & this could only be comforting. She liked anxious people.

The voice said, Everything made by the hand of man is either ugly or beautiful.

Difficult to know what to say to that. Difficult to contradict a man who was known to do it to himself.

ii

All the listening faces, & somewhere among their number her brother. The large panelled room was full & the gathering inclined to the fashionable. How could it be that the outfits were so unusual—there were velvet & fur collars, & feathered ones—yet everyone looked alike?

She was today fortunate to have no more regard for resembling her neighbour than she had inclination to ask them to dance—& there was Otho, in the front row, of course. He would, as he did everything, be sure to question her late arrival.

& it might as well be beautiful as well as ugly, came the voice onstage.

Hastening to her seat & imagining herself to be invisible, halfway along the row she tripped, making not one but several apologies. A murmur audible & a flame in her cheeks as the man she had come to hear, without a pause in his delivery, tilted his head to make her the centre of attention.

To make it all the worse, Otho was rising to greet her.*

Constance wondered why she hadn't stayed at home. All day preparing to go out to turn around & go home again. For being out was not as marvellous as people would have had you believe.

& before her, this OW was only a little overdressed. Either his waistcoat didn't fit or he was a bit fat, & his hands as he spoke were dusting an invisible sideboard. All things considered, he was very nice to look at. But she hardly looked at him at all, she hardly listened to him; she just took comfort in being seated & out of view.

OW leaned—on the air?—before accelerating his delivery, as though energised by her presence. Could this be the case? Until this moment, she had felt uncertain & yet quite

---

* You were in silhouette. Only when you pushed along the row did your face find the light.

determined, a discrepancy that had got her only as far as an unfamiliar room to hear a voice less resonant than the one she was expecting.

When I enter a room, I see a carpet of vulgar pattern, a cracked plate upon the wall, with a peacock feather stuck behind it…

Doubts emerged as to whether he was aware of her presence, & if she should do anything to bring attention to herself, whether she should have brought a fan or an eyeglass. A fan would have been just the thing in here, for the room could have done with an airing. Much boiled breath suspended in the air smelling the place up.*

I sit down upon a badly glued machine-made chair that creaks upon being touched. I turn to look for the beauties of nature.

Those words occupied the scant few feet between her & OW. But within the deliciousness of sentences an uneasiness, attractive at that, lay concealed. For there could be no denying his eloquence or that on its own such stimulating talk was insufficient. Some things in life were best expressed in words—instructions or complaints, requests for directions or to noisy neighbours to pipe down—& some were not.

A good rule to follow in a house is to have nothing therein but what is useful or beautiful.

---

*You interrupted my story. Very little attention was paid to my forbearance. The room was yours.

She arranged herself more comfortably. In the absence of the corset, she would have to learn to sit up straight.

Constance had not very much use for the word beautiful. Being born beautiful was hardly evidence of any kind of talent, was it? It was a sign of good luck & nothing more. So easy & so tempting to allow your face to carry you into & out of difficult situations. Good bones, symmetry & an inviting smile accruing something supernatural.

The question of whether Constance herself was beautiful occupied her more than it should have. This morning she had thought so, tilting her chin & standing slant before the mirror to give the impression of great conviction in herself. The problem was, on other mornings all she saw when she looked in the mirror was a witch with a thick snout. & she wondered now if OW would be able to notice anything else.

Had he looked to her at the delivery of the line? Perhaps he had. Perhaps he had. That her approval was of very little consequence to anyone didn't stop her from giving a firm nod in response to this remark, the last OW made before he deserted the stage.

A grumbling to her side. Even though they were being slowly submerged under a wave of applause, she felt its force; Otho was not impressed.

All that over a bit of decorating, he said.*

Her brother in his wisdom was rising to leave. Constance, a little diminished by OW's departure, was about to follow

---

* I'll have you know that kind of eloquence isn't dashed off overnight.

when a porter arrived with a note & a smile which may have said, not only have I read this, I implore you to accept the invitation.

The note was addressed 'To a decorative young woman', who was being invited for after-show refreshments.

Had it been dictated or written in a hurry? she wondered. How did he have the time?

Otho had his eyes on her.

There was also the matter of her oafish brother tramping along after her.

You're giving very little away, he said.

Am I?

What do you make of him?

I really don't know.

Oh, I think you do. Suffice to say he was rather too flamboyant for my liking.

Didn't she know only too well what her brother was getting at? Wasn't it nice, not to mention important, to have some things hidden? She was apt to keeping secrets—that was putting it mildly—& she hadn't had a good one in a long time. The best ones, which were to do with love, felt as though there was a commotion of flowers budding wild inside of her. She couldn't be sure if actual tendrils weren't twining in & out of her ribs. But there was a lot one person could carry.

& do you know, at Oxford he was known to be an aesthete.

In that case, Constance said, my mind has been polluted with matters aesthetic.

The well-worn veil that was being placed over her sunny outlook. & no need to ask the meaning of flamboyant.

The likes of OW lived in a show that neither incorporated nor required the presence of any Constance Lloyds. To that story there was very little to add. Her days were spent occupying the wings. & she had long been unwilling to spend any more time there. So what was it about the invitation that made her not want to accept it?

To the porter she said, Would you say that I am delighted to receive his invitation & I'd be pleased to make his acquaintance another time.

iii

What was it about Mayfair that attracted the light? Both sides of Park Street were awash in excessive sunshine. & no day this to be finding oneself so dazzled.

In this soaring afternoon would there be found her future? That was the question. Nothing less than love with no limit.*

Beside her—when was he not?—trotted Otho, carrying himself as if the afternoon were there for the taking.

You've made an effort.

Possibly too much of one, she said.

No quibbles there.

But I don't want to seem at all pushy.

---

* You do get yourself in some awful pickles, my dear.

Thus said the pushy young woman.

Constance did not take kindly to the comment & to the insinuation that she was somewhat unwound, just as she had not been taking kindly to her own thoughts. For she had been thinking of herself in the most peculiar ways, as being destined to consume her own flesh. Some nights she would find herself taken over by imaginings, wherein she was being passed around a room full of young men avid for her flesh. Could one spoil from a fantasy? That was the other question.* There was the hard fact of her virginity, & that there was more wildness in her than in a young wolf.

I say, said Otho, in no imitation of a dandy. I hope they'll take me as they find me.

They shall have to.

Rather than being there as an escort, Otho seemed to think the invitation was in his name. The card in *her* hand read:

> The pleasure of your company is requested At Home with Lady Jane Wilde, Park Street, Mayfair. Saturdays 5–7 p.m. RSVP.

If only, as wasn't proper, she could have gone alone. How much more thrilling would it have been? & she felt downhearted at the prospect, but then—as there would be plenty of time to be downhearted later, at home, with nothing

---

* Not to my knowledge.

but a mildewed aunt & a mute grandfather for company—she tried to talk herself out of it.

Her outfit, innocuous enough at first sight, had earlier been the source of much debate. Aunt Emily had remarked that she looked like a farmhand.

What makes you think that isn't my intention?

Did you intend to get dressed in such a hurry?

Emily was never intentionally droll. But such words as Constance could think of she had kept to herself. & having objected to the day dress, Emily gave her approval to some hooped affair that was everything the day dress was not. Constance, with Dolly at the ready to help with the crinoline, knew not to argue the point.*

A show was made then of having Dolly turn the chests upside down, with Constance trying on everything she owned. To much throat-clearing from Emily, off came the perfectly dull & acceptable thing she was wearing. Her ghastly get-up (thank you, dear Otho).

Was it such a crime to be able to move your arm in what you wore? What if she would be required to bowl a ball or paint a picture? But her aunt would not be told that a crinoline was a fire hazard. & what if she were to fall under the wheels of a carriage? It was like walking around with a building attached to you.

On went far too much silk & satin, all before covering everything under this cloak. Now she would have to

---

* That in itself should go down as a victory.

remember to fall in with the right company, & to speak a little but not too much. What else? Admire but don't overpraise the furnishings. & avoid the sandwiches, which were known to be the worst in London.

iv

A scruffy maid directed them with a jerk of the thumb towards the parlour.

In there with you.

The gall.

But the house & the sorry state it was in soon cured Constance of her nerves. In the doorway holding the old place up was OW. As if by some bureaucratic miscalculation, or he were holding it for a bet, there was a teapot in his hand. & behind him, in defiance of the swathes of sunshine in the street, the drawing room was bathed in candlelight. How would they get anything done with the curtains drawn in the afternoon?

& another optical illusion, no more OW. All that was missing was the puff of smoke.

In the gloom of the parlour, the gathering was well under way. She found herself marooned in the centre of the room, with no one familiar, not even her brother, in view. Faces turned in every direction but hers. & what a relief to see that no one seemed to be enjoying themselves.

How convenient that every dreary person in London could

be found in the one room. Ah, there was Otho, at a messy sideboard, from where he was returning with a candle. What were the chances of him falling over someone or something on his way back?

I would be more inclined to mingle if I could see where I was going, he said.

The candle was handed to her just as OW passed, on wings, carrying that teapot from somewhere to somewhere. Not that he'd poured anyone a cup from it. He was just carrying it around.

A thought seemed to be occurring to him. A moment's standstill followed, a sense of uncertainty singing between them.*

Tea?

With one hand holding her candle, Constance held a cupped palm under the spout.

Perhaps we could start with a cup? she said.

Very, very well observed.

In this phrase, he was all she wanted him to be: a gentle man attempting to make her welcome in his home.

There was this man & there was OW—but she did not see them as separate beings.

For Constance had decided. There would be no other. For she knew that OW was so enamoured of beauty, decoration, artists, architects, interiors, opulence. & she was today to discover that there was so much he had to say about the world.

---

* All it took was your face in candlelight.

He had more to say on commonplace subjects than anyone she knew; he could at the drop of a pin discourse on the tea-having habits of the inhabitants of cities where he had gone on all his tours, the movement towards public tearooms, even a woman's right to frequent them.

Wasn't OW proving himself to be the kindest of men? & hadn't she heard for herself that he was a gifted writer? He seemed to have great plans for himself anyway, & so much the better if from time to time she might be held in high enough regard to be made part of those plans.

She had decided.

She was minded to ask him to continue pouring the tea, just to see what he would have done. It might have been worth the scalding. & she imagined him making her a bandage from that dirty towel. & they would together drink tea—sharing the cup—& in her mind the taste would be as delicious & stimulating as any port or champagne. This, of course, seemed like the beginnings of a ridiculous fantasy. & Constance was shocked, standing there before a stranger, who seemed kindly but might not have been, that she was allowing herself to be animated by something that wasn't real. It seemed suddenly plausible, or not implausible. Taking shape in her mind was a picture of a couple kissing in a bedroom dark like this room or in a churchyard soaked in blossom & bright sunshine.

& the longer she considered it, the more appealing it became, & the source of its appeal was, at the time, due to it being a fantasy & no more.

He certainly looked younger & less grand than at the Prince's Hall. His teeth for such a young man were the colour of curry powder. Less assured of gait & of bearing, he was—by her reckoning, what counted for it—much more reachable, more subdued, & more attractive. More himself.

One can only be oneself at home; she told herself that. What's more, he looked like he belonged to no one. She told herself that.

You need good eyes in this light, she said.

He held her gaze before taking the candle from her & returning it to the sideboard.

v

Inevitable, was it not, that the parlour would have its own hapless bearing. The rooms were as small as the Ws were large.

Impossible to say in this brown light if it was night or day. A huddle of dining chairs faced the wall where scaffolding held up a listing & too-busy mantelpiece. & there was, not that Constance could have given them names, the smell of boiled vegetables. Or was it of a chamber pot? This could have been the carpets; they did not look promising.

LJW was stout enough to have been mistaken for the armchair in which she sat. The alcove afforded her a perfect view of all the goings-on at ankle level & thereabouts. Some flowers had been left in their paper, & Constance was appalled

& not a little amused by the abject posture of a towel that had been left drying on an abandoned music stand.

Constance had to bend to hear her say, I see you have made Oscar's acquaintance already. An idler, as you've seen. But lazy in the most natural & admirable of ways.

OW appeared, bearing tea on a tray. Constance took it with murmured thanks & no mention of there being as much liquid in the saucer as in the cup.

Miss Lloyd, may I properly present my son, The Oscar Wilde, which it is his destiny to become. Let us both pray that his penchant for overdrawing the tea will not impede his glide through the world of letters.

LJW's mother tongue was gibberish.

All three, like fortune-tellers, stared into their cups, until LJW said, On its own I find tea tends to the wet.

OW rubbed his face.

He didn't seem to make the inference. The moment turning then, & something posthumous—ashen almost—about the three of them, as though they had gathered to commemorate a loved one, but had forgotten who. More examination of the contents of her cup.*

LJW looked up at her son.

We won't keep you.

Oh, I was hoping that you would.

The garibaldis, dear?

Of course, Mama. One moment, Miss Lloyd.

---

* You were always so stubborn in your silences.

Constance, instead of being bereft at his departure, found herself able to relax a little.

All teapot & no cup, LJW said. All he thrives on is discipline.

A survey was made of the room. By the window, evidently desperate for daylight, was a group of young victims to fashion—demure, bored & boring—by whom Constance could feel herself being appraised.

Now let's see, said LJW. Where shall we put you? You might find some fruitful discourse among the peeresses.

A list a yard long of the reasons why Constance had no wish to join their number.

The veil of disgust she wore was not directed at the assembled but at herself & her inability to simultaneously discourse on seventeen different subjects.

She would take her lesson & keep quiet.

Elsewhere in the room, next to a thicket of men in ecclesiastical garb, was an earnest grouping of young poets. OW ignored them on his way to refill the cups, & the saucers, of the rich young ladies. She would not have been surprised to have found Otho among their number, angling for an invitation home.

LJW continued, We are fortunate to attract a good number of young radicals, although you would want to know your own mind. I'm sure you could hold your own. Or there's always Oscar. Who pours tea very well, don't you think?

It was as though Constance were being shown how to ride a bicycle without stabilisers. & she was grateful for the lesson & that she was able to float past the outstretched hand of a dreary-looking poet. Her tea had not been drunk—was it floor sweepings it tasted of?—& she handed the cup to a harried-looking OW, who pantomimed looking around for help.

The butler is known for his unauthorised absences.

I noticed, Constance said.

& what else did you notice, Miss Lloyd? I see your eyes swaying this way & that.

I noticed that you paid more attention to the heiresses than the poets. & I noticed also how sweet you were to your mother. In fact I couldn't help but observe that in conversation with her you're far less affected than you are in public.

It's my misfortune to have presented such a façade to the world.

I don't much go in for façades. But entirely necessary in your field, I'm sure.

But not here, not at home. & how do you find us, Miss Lloyd?

An inch of daylight was peeping through the curtains. Enough to tickle her feet & no more. Constance did not remark upon the frayed upholstery. Nor did she give in to the realisation that the candlelight must have been there to disguise the shabbiness.

Now she had it. The lion's head on OW was misleading. The poor fellow was nervous as a kitten, she was certain of it, for she could hear him agreeing with everything that was said to him & doing anything to move the conversation along. She watched him pour tea & spill tea & engage in all kinds of conversations—the Borgias, the kangaroos in London Zoo, the skin on rice pudding—as if entertaining some bored & judgemental god.

She tried to determine what had made him so eager to please. & it was eagerness itself that made Constance consider the possibilities: hints of brightness, & charm, but being quite anxious about it, for his expression changed several times a second.

There it was, there he was.

OW returned to his mother's side with more tea, which was awful, & appeared as comforting to them as their own bathwater. To keep them all amused, he told one church warden a story about a parish priest in Tipperary who had fathered seven children. It was agreed that they would all say a prayer for the children.

What an unusual evening it was proving to be. No struggle to imagine this as the perfect environment in which a young man would develop his wit. She found herself certain that, rather than falling into the same mire—the most forsaken mire a person could ever be caught in—mutual loneliness left both parties more open to love. Would she have been as open to it if she had been cocooned in it since childhood? No wit in the world could have convinced her differently.

OW had sensed this from her. How could he have missed it? But without any sense of herself, she was even less sure of who he was & how he might well fail to pick her out from all the darling & attentive heiresses.

With her brother hovering & OW so far from hand, all that happened was that she felt even more alone. There was no other word than alone. & how her wits were failing her. She was not ready to go but she was unable to stay. Oh, she was going to offer to stay, & was going to give herself a reason to by putting on a uniform to clear up the cups, picking them up & putting them onto a tray. & wasn't this what she meant by being open to love?

Once the less favoured had taken their leave, Constance found herself with an audience of one. OW was arranging all the available candles around the chair where she sat reading a manuscript entitled *The House Beautiful.**

How she tried her best to accommodate this anxious altar boy before her. As a stance, kneeling was quite something. His eyes were willing her to read on. Was he trying to find something in her face? On she read, with OW mouthing the words to himself.

I don't know if it's the lighting or the lack of tea, she said. But I can hardly concentrate.

She gave a meek laugh as her words petered out.

I'd like you to keep it.

Keep it? No, certainly not.

OW was waiting for her to say something else. Otho could be heard in the hall, hands in pockets probably, chest out, complaining about the state of the roads in Bayswater.

Intimacy in her experience was make-believe & finding

* It was my only copy.

it a matter of luck, but this was a felt moment. & few & far between were these felt moments.

He was examining her so closely. Inches from her feet one finger traced a slant line in the air.

Might I suggest that you limit the use of the word beautiful? It loses its impact on the sixth or seventh instance.

vi

The slamming of the door made Constance feel as though she had done something wrong. Such was the force of it that the sky, much the same startling colour as before, shook, & Constance called out, I beg your pardon! That she spoke so cheerily made no difference. It was her wont, & had been forever, to offer apologies in situations—to her aunt this morning, for example—that ill required one.

Had it been the way in which she had monopolised OW's company, or the way in which he had read to her aloud from his manuscript, following her around the room at one point, or the way in which he had congratulated her, quite unnecessarily, on her way of eating a garibaldi? Eating a garibaldi was eating a garibaldi, was it not?

Or perhaps the maid directed venom at all the departing guests?

Well, Constance had seen where the women worked—she had a great deal to be angry about. She could not altogether be blamed.

A sideways look at the parlour windows. Now would have been the time for the curtains to be flung open. The windows, were they ever opened? Could they have been? A house like that, if it could have expressed itself, would have wanted to scream out pain, & the scream would have kept going for some time. A fumigation really wouldn't have gone amiss.

She hadn't been able to get out of there quickly enough, & now Constance wanted to go straight back inside. For she was losing control of herself, & she was elated, with nothing to link the two.

The evening at the Wildes' had been none too scary, but the other side of it was that she cared about soirées about as much as she cared for seeing Grandfather's turds floating in the bowl. There was no need to make too much of it.

They were minutes by foot from the park. She needed to see some green, & feel the response of the grass; the earth, breathing. Whenever she joined the Lord, this was all she wanted with her. Sweet grass, a breeze through it, little more would be necessary.

So that was the famous Oscar Wilde, Otho said. But tell me truly, what's he famous for?

Being himself? she said.

Are you having your head turned?

She could very well have conceded the point.

If a tightrope had been strung over the Serpentine, she would have got up & walked on it. Constance Lloyd may have been/may not have been falling in love.

It's staying exactly where it is, she said.

vii

Oscar was every day turning up in a different coat. News had come from America & he was to be off there again to speak for much money; thus every walk they took was of necessity endowed with consequence.

One damp day in late spring, he came to call on her so that they might take a walk—tiptoeing, almost, to add significance—so that they could pass comment on all the other courtships playing out in Hyde Park.

Whose idea was it to take another stroll in the park? Hers as much as his, she supposed. More than once she was reminded that a courtship was a dance towards a marriage bound around the real stuff, which was the sex that was sure to beget a child, perhaps frequent sex & more than one child.

Do you like it that I'm Irish? she said.

You're not really, are you? Very Irish.

As much as you are.

Not very then.

But the next burst of talkativeness had its roots in a Longford cemetery. Oscar was not an only child; she had assumed he was. There was a little sister who died, the nonentity as real to him as the young elms in the park. The sadness quite real too, grief live in him still, for how could you escape the image of the golden-haired corpse* & the young pallbearer?

* Now I wonder did I ever withhold anything at all from you?

She was relieved when he stopped crying. It had gone on so much that he'd had to blow his nose with her handkerchief. Her suitor was a sad child &, damp hanky in hand, she was beginning to dread what was left of the outing. At the gates of the park, passing a young tree with boughs growing out & up in all directions, she made a solemn decision, if not to ignore the versions of young love on show in the park then to consider herself & Oscar as the elected leaders of the tribe, for she had decided that this was the only way to go about being alive & in love—that if you are not the only one going through it, you are going through the best possible version of it.

The path under them had been softened by a shower of rain. The sour air, she could feel spores on her, & the park with its greenness & brownness was not much of a place for lovers.

It was not a place for lovers but for all London & the world.

Behold a legion of saintly young governesses, proceeding in the manner of gaolers emptying corridors of a night. Was there one child in London capable of walking a straight line? & were all the young women of such a sullen disposition? Were the witty, non-morbs children being kept indoors? One lay on the damp ground, like a dead bee. Another one, the first one's big brother, stood by, berating him in the manner of a preacher.

She would without a worry have flung them all—dead bees & preachers—into the lake.

Spring, she said. People must be glad of the fresh air.

She had said much the same thing when he picked her

up this afternoon. The smell of damp earth & manure was becoming the smell of love. She believed that to be true for everyone there & only more so for her & Oscar.

Aren't you going to say one thing?

Oscar roused himself eventually to say, Quite.

Was it for fear it might excite her that he would back away from any talk that might be considered too interesting? On their walks, he liked to slow & point out a spectacle that was hardly worth the pointing out. A solemn child, an ordinary dog. & wasn't it that London had been through a week that would have drowned a seal? & wasn't it that the overflowing drains were playing havoc with the plumbing at Park Street? She thought she would keel over when Oscar started in on that.

They could have been talking about love, but they were talking about plumbing. For a full tour of the lake that's all she could think of. LJW on the toilet.

She thought her heart might burst then, when she saw him fumble in his inside pocket for the bit of paper he consulted before continuing.

They were, according to The Oscar Wilde, about to take flight & sail the skies of love.

Oh dear.

But he had been unhappy too with all the talk of drains, & she gave a full sigh as he began that eulogy to flight, as though to sail along in those skies might diminish the private, fuzzy feeling—& the fuzzies, as vague & warm as a gas, were all that were pushing her one more time around the park.

Oscar put away his bit of paper—she hadn't heard a word he had said, preferring to imagine the gas canister being stowed out of sight & well out of her reach. The daunting & impossible job of finding it was now a certainty—the emptiness she feared was already on her, the fuzzies had long departed through the Coalbrookdale Gates & all she was left with was the smell of grass & dung.

Summer will be soon, she said.

It wouldn't have been much to reply.

She longed all of a sudden for him to be gone to America already. For Constance was smothered by his looming departure yet stung by this dull talk & these long silences.

All the ripostes in the world when they were in company, of course. But here in the bloody park they were neither on show nor alone, &, as if in his mind he were busy herding elephants, Oscar had very little to say for himself. It was not hard to imagine them growing too used to one another.

& were they thinking the same thing, that whether it made any sense or not they should at one time or another be married? Once you had decided upon someone, you could hardly undecide.*

Constance went on.

I found your mother to be very interesting.

Whenever she deigns to join us on this planet.

It must be nice to live at one remove from the world.

---

* Something in me sinks, & keeps sinking, at the thought. I have never had anyone like you. I never shall again.

My mother is far too much in love with the world to want to be away from it.

She walked away, reminding him that, You can save that kind of talk for one of your lectures. It won't work on me.

If they could make it through one normal conversation today, they could get through anything.

Straying onto the grass, Oscar suggested they might sit for a moment. There was a fine patch which he chose to avoid, for it was occupied by a silly little terrier. Oscar was scared. Although the dog was staring at them, it was as if politely & without any intent. There, its gaze was fixed on another dog, some kind of prissy spaniel. The terrier paused, went stock-still then launched itself at the poor spaniel.

It was to Constance quite like watching a squabble over the curlers at the ladies' hairdressers. But Oscar was shielding his eyes. He was in no mood to be ribbed about it either. But she could not trust herself not to laugh.

Off he went.

To go after him, Constance found herself doubling back, off the path & in something of a fever at the base of the elm that was most certainly not for climbing on.

She was unusually aroused but couldn't very well say so. Up the tree with her so. Some traction was to be found on the trunk before ushering herself onto & along the branch. She sat with her chest heaving, watching all the toing & froing below. Her vision was such that the governesses seemed docile & the children placid.

Even Oscar looked so much less commanding from up here. In not being able to hear what he was saying, she was able to observe the two great poles of his personality: swagger & shyness. Either he would be not speaking or he would be coming back with a spiel about sailing in the sky that would be too confident & courteous by half.

He stood at the foot of the tree, with an exhausted look to him.

I say, you resemble a mountain goat.

What are you waiting for? she said.

In the end, she had to haul him up beside her. What a sight his wagging legs must have made. & there they sat, Constance with a foxy grin, legs swinging like a little girl who had gotten away with something she shouldn't have.

Are you aware, she said, of one of the joys of being up here?

It's not down there?

Oscar's face was a death-mask of anxiety.

No one can see us.

His hand was white from holding on to the branch. A perfect moment then for Constance, who was working from no plan, to take his hand, so soft to touch, & to steal a kiss on his cheek.

They were in love, but thankfully not too much. Constance had wanted a lover's place in the pecking order, without a lover's problems. & that she had no business in being so forward as to climb a tree to excite her man was exactly the point. She could make out the rim of the park & the railings—& wasn't it amusing that it resembled a prison of sorts?

She looked again & saw herself behind the railings, & not only was she unable to get out from behind them, the bars were closing in.

She turned her face upwards, so that all she saw were leaves & sky. Even Oscar was invisible. Now she felt like pretending nothing had happened. But there it was, the shape of her lips imprinted on his face.

Was it as easy as all that?

A hooray went up then, from the trio of men having their ham sandwiches on the bench below. Constance was left in no doubt that they had been observed.

Is this what it's like to be a performer? she said.

Oscar's expression was conceding nothing.*

Of course he then had to put their kiss into words, conjuring for her certain admiration the image of a nervous flower.

A flower? she said.

Quite.

Even when an insoluble moment had overtaken them, even then Oscar was able to wrench out of himself an overspun simplification.**

Their kissing—by all means warm & sweet, but not at all straightforward—was being summarised as if it had been foreseen. Was there something so lacking in an intimate experience that it could be described so fully & with such ease? Of all that they were, kisses were their own language, the

---

* Would this be as good as we'd ever get it?

** Do tell me what's wrong with flowers. For you know very well that it is only a simplification when it is something you don't want to hear.

first the sweetest & hardest to decipher—cryptic, & aspiring to possess the known characteristic of repeating itself. & what chance did Oscar have against a kiss that was orchestrated to test & to flatter? Their only expression was to be found in relation to other kisses & were themselves possessed of the dishonesty of an organism that was only ever half formed &, until it met another, erred to think of itself as complete.

viii

The pleasures of Dublin.

But everyone—or Constance—was in a bad humour on account of the season. Dark all day & staying that way. She was standing near the window but not by it & scarcely dared to look out of it anyway, in case Oscar appeared & saw that she had been waiting in for him. Or that in a dead & anxious state she had been reading & reading again his letters.

Her blood was as thick as pouring tarmacadam, for she was as confused as she could be. The imaginative & daring man who had been lecturing all week at the Gaiety was indeed the same man his mother had been referring to. *The* Oscar Wilde's reputation was rising as ominously as a flood on the Liffey. But the entire town was climbing over itself to catch sight of a man she didn't herself recognise.

Constance was in a love affair with several men. Put her Oscar before a crowded auditorium in London or Dublin or Baton Rouge, with all the respectable folk of the town hanging on his every word, & he would poise himself, one foot perpendicular to the other, before delivering his take on the decorative arts with an eloquence that moved through her like some repellent liquid.

Now that she knew him, Oscar—in person—was constrained & soggy-seeming, & with his grotty manuscripts tucked under his elbow as unthreatening & lovely as a cup of cocoa.

& she had been standing in the one place for days.

He had been due that morning as well as the morning before & the morning before that.

When she was little, God was a word she could never say. Sex was a word she could never say. Together they could not even be contemplated. Now she was old enough to understand, or not understand, the two joined together as a secret murmur in her soul. It was becoming more difficult to distinguish one from another. That they seemed to her reconcilable was something she knew to keep to herself. Or if it was to be shared with anyone, the Oscar Wildes of this world, it would be as acknowledgement of what they already knew. It might have been different if she had been born a man.

She would keep God in her heart, she decided. The wariness of sex came from somewhere else. For love was not one thing, & sex was never merely sex. However it went, it would take a bit of getting over & getting used to. However, composing herself was what she did. Composed was what she was.

Oscar was staying around the corner in the Shelbourne,

from where there came notes that she read over & over without being able to decipher them.

There was YET ANOTHER OSCAR—the Oscar of the page was another creature altogether.

She had on her Jaeger wool coat, so that if he did appear—he wouldn't, would he?—she could say that she was on her way out for a walk on miserable Stephen's Green, in the rain if she had to, & he would have to call back another day.

Otho had said, hadn't he? That she could have gone to meet him at the theatre. But she had seen him perform so many times, & all Constance wanted was for them to be alone. One of him & one of her.

Dolly, who had been on alert all morning, came in wearing a familiar expression of helplessness.*

Oscar appeared &, with a vacant smile on his face, said, What do you say to a stroll?

Constance removed her coat & said she was staying where she was. It made no difference that he was watching her as attentively as ever.

---

* How late was I? Do you know what I was trying to do? I was trying to convince the young rascal in the hotel to provide me with a kipper while I rehearsed my speech. I was reliably informed that breakfast was eight till nine. Sir! An egg or two wouldn't go amiss, I said, if there are no more kippers, which do tend to repeat on you. Not at all what I wanted from my afternoon. Breakfast is eight till nine, sir, came the refrain. The young fellow seemed to cherish that information. That settled it then; I didn't want kippers & the young man couldn't give them to me. Wasn't I only trying to distract myself from my speech? Why on earth was I bothering trying to impress you? That's an impossibility. I wouldn't try it now.

Very well, he said. That is much more what I had in mind. More conducive to… You didn't come to the theatre. Why ever not?

Haven't I heard it before?

It's never the same twice, he said.

In your prolonged absence, I took a chance to reread some of your old letters. I must say you're much more articulate on the page. & may I ask the meaning of this bit? 'From the moment I met you I loved you, loved you blindly, adoringly, madly. You did not know it then—you know it now.'

She put the letter away, as though for further consideration, before turning to the window that had been reflecting her dissatisfaction back to her all morning. A walk on Stephen's Green had been on the cards—she was not exactly gleeful at the prospect—& if it was to be rainy, which it would be, Oscar had had other vague ideas about taking tea at his hotel. They could forget about all that now.

Did you need blindly, adoringly & madly? she said. & don't you think you overdo it?

I know I overuse certain words.

Whatever it is you're going to say, I might have entertained the preamble this morning. Now I'd really rather you got on with it.

Was that a twitch arising in his face? His features were not normally so mobile; now everything was on the move.

He made a move towards her but she shooed him away, even though she liked what he had on, a subtle & sweet cologne that gave her ideas of Italy, & a desire that they could leave Ireland & England & all the rain—& their families—forever.

Stay where you are, she said.

She was walking the most involved figures of eight around him now. Not her intention to flummox him, but that appeared to have been the end result. It was a small price to pay for having been kept waiting.

I know I overuse certain words, he said. But I also know that what I am about to say I have never said before & I am certain never to say again. I have never knowingly disobeyed an impulse as strong as the one that overcomes me now.

Which Oscar was this now? Not the one she had spent all that time waiting for. How could she say—she simply couldn't—that she would like him to express himself better? Oh, let him be, was the answer. Let a person be.

Are you or aren't you overcome? Explain yourself.

I know I overuse certain words.

For goodness' sake, she said. Clever people are such exhausting company. Thankfully you're only clever in public. & if you're here to propose marriage, let's get on with it.

She took a step back. He took a step back.

Now that was a surprise, she said.

Constance stood still so that Oscar could approach her. She held out her hand for his & considered the facts.

The leaving of home, Ireland & England, had been her goal, but the chance of a proposal—today—had not crossed her mind AT ALL. She had been neither expecting it nor was she taken by surprise. But it was too late to make that enigma clear. & had she made things even worse by agreeing to one she was not even certain had been on the cards?

What does one say after that? he said.

You tell me.

You will be my wife?

Her answer was a nod of the head, which Oscar interpreted as an invitation to close his eyes & peck her cheek.

A ring appeared then, & in a rush of real surprise & delight & a little despair, at what she didn't know, Constance found herself smiling. The ring was a heart formed from diamonds, rather small, enclosing two pearls. None too showy at all.

Oscar was LEARNING.

Was it the moment for another kiss, a FLURRY of them?

Soon they would be free to do whatever they wanted. & if The Oscar Wilde had meant to propose*—the ring had hardly been found in the gutters of Ely Square—& if really & truly she had wanted him to, there would be more to worry about than kissing. Ever since that day in Hyde Park his advances had grown ever more tentative & apologetic &, to her, inflammatory, perhaps as a communication from one to the other, from him to her, that even the having of DESIRES was going TOO FAR.

---

* The intent was there, let me assure you. Those who have known new love will recognise that was then doomed to being the hopeful sort. & it was in this spirit that I went about the making & getting of a ring. Wondering, in the doing, if you were as hopeful as I was. I am quite ready to say that I think you were.

Do you trust me to put this on your finger? he said.

Not a whit.

ix

The excitements of Ireland soon faded.

With Oscar having been & gone, & several times, on his speaking engagements, there were overdue matters to attend to in London. Normally Constance would regard herself as TOO INDEPENDENT to have to explain her intentions to anyone. But when it came to the matter of her family allowance, a certain amount of dependence would have to be acknowledged & some explaining would have to be done.

That Oscar regarded talking to her family as an inconvenience meant they had had to do several go-arounds of the park while she convinced him that presenting himself for inspection by her grandfather & her aunt was a good idea.

Was it for this reason that Constance felt the need to knock on her own front door? & if she could have stopped her heartbeat she would have, for it was drowning out the knock. Seeing Dolly's face would help, she thought. Today's expression might be her usual helplessness with a dash of Dutch courage.*

---

* Dolly, could I interest you in visiting my cell? I have some things that need doing.

Otho, who had made a point of being there to answer the door, showed no interest in making their visitor AT ALL welcome. He rustled around in his pockets & uselessly adjusted a lamp before disappearing to fetch Aunt Emily & Grandfather. His officiousness was in keeping with her nerves &, she vowed, would have to be explained later.

Plain sailing thus far, Oscar said.

He was wearing one of the frock coats he wore to perform in, which was offset by a pink face from a night on the wine. He looked good but he stank. & she wished he would suppress the urge to impress everyone. The Lloyds were not the kind of people to be impressed by anyone.

The flowers that had been arriving daily while he was away had been enough to cement his reputation, in her aunt's eyes, as decadent. Emily took daily pleasure in commenting on the way in which flowers decayed. All that money for something that would be thrown away.

Keep that coat done up, Constance said. Things are liable to get frosty.

In the drawing room, Oscar whispered that the arrangement of the two dining chairs facing a couch was as foreboding as a courtroom. Seated before them were Emily & Otho. Officiating over proceedings, without giving any indication that he wasn't asleep, was her grandfather.

To meet Horatio Lloyd for the first time was to think someone had for a bet dressed up a waxwork & sat it in an armchair & given it tea. Only the raising of the cup to his lips gave the indication that he was alive. He frightened people, children especially.*

Grandfather was sizing Oscar up, the coat & everything. But he was forever making calculations that he kept to himself. It had been some time since anything had been put into words. All messages were sent from his eyes—which were soaked in aspic—& a forefinger pointed in a certain direction. The ceiling meant yes. The floor meant no. It was in a terrible & morbs way a state worth aspiring to.

Between them, her grandfather never spoke, & her aunt hardly said anything nice. &, within moments of taking her seat, it was clear to Constance that her brother was not about to deliver any speeches welcoming Oscar into the family.

Aunt Emily had not greeted him but saw fit to address Oscar as you would a chimney sweep.

You're a theatrical person, she said. A showman, is it?**

No 'how was your trip?' Whose idea had it been for Emily to speak first? The showman question was asked without curiosity, & in her aunt's tone was irritation & possibly venom.

Constance was for the first time compelled to answer on Oscar's behalf.

Not as such, Aunt.

Her Oscar was no more a showman than he was that chimney sweep.

---

* Can we get back to the boys? I'm worried over your reports of Vyvyan. How is his Italian?

** Guilty as charged.

The others were having tea, but NO REFRESHMENTS had been offered to Constance or Oscar. She felt like going downstairs & coming up with a plate of cream buns for the pair of them.

She tried to catch his eye—to offer reassurance & wordlessly to express this silly idea about the buns—but Oscar's gaze meanwhile had travelled to the floor.

Grandfather didn't get out much, & the wearing of woollen slippers kept things simple. There followed a long & meaningful look in the direction of his feet. She thought for a moment Oscar might say something. Even though she could know nothing of what he was thinking, she was glad he was keeping it to himself. When it came to Oscar, one never assumed. & would he have stopped at the slippers?

Constance looked about her. Certainly there would be a lot for Oscar to critique. The wasteland of oak, lamps that couldn't illuminate a forty-foot room, a baffled-looking mantel clock that hadn't once kept the right time & in the way of an owl that couldn't hoot was now being entirely left to its own devices.

We haven't had many showmen around here, Emily said.

Oscar was evidently taken aback by Emily's reaction to him or, more likely, the preconceptions with which she had entered the room & was sharing to her left & right.

Writer is really quite easy to say.

Until he spoke up for himself, Constance had rarely seen Oscar at ANYONE'S mercy.

His response might have been made more acute by the presence of his hangover, which though it had gone unremarked upon was all too apparent. She had felt it in the soupiness of his kiss & could see it now in the sweat on his temples. But Constance disapproved of aggressive aunts a lot more than she did of soupy kisses & sweaty temples.

Do you have any documentation to that effect? said Otho.

My face on a hundred posters.*

I think you're having us on.

Emily & Otho were overlapping, but it was Grandfather, who hadn't said a word, & wouldn't, that Oscar was most watchful of. For it was her grandfather's approval for the marriage they were seeking.

Mister Lloyd? If they could supply me with ink & a pen, I could write you a sonnet.

Constance laughed, chastising herself for it. As often happened with him when he had been away performing, Oscar's delivery was a little much. & the Lloyds were not a paying audience.

Expect all this to be yours for a poem, do you? Otho said. Is that what this is?

Aunt Emily said, Mister Wilde. We would like to ask Constance a few questions. & in order to do that it would be better if we had her to ourselves.

---

* Were there not all these reminders of whomever the world thought me to be, I might have been inclined to forget it myself.

x

It had only been when her mother had remarried that Constance was cast away to the thick walls & expensive quiet of 100 Lancaster Gate.

There may once have been a time when she missed THE TOUCH OF A MATERNAL HAND. But the indifference cultivated in the English nursery had found its thoroughbred in Ada Atkinson. Young Constance had on more than one occasion been given her porridge in the dog's bowl. The much-adored dog.

& how could she forget her forearm giving in to the heat of the fire-iron, her skin crackling like the pork of Sunday roast?

But Mama's cruelty was something she dared not stir up too much by too much reminiscing. The odd thing was that it all felt completely normal. Not only that, she had decided that her mother was deserving of gratitude. Perhaps it was all good preparation for the humiliation to which she was about to be submitted.

The ability to withstand pain was the most valuable part of the Atkinson family legacy.

She wanted to ask them all to leave, but she couldn't. She couldn't for Constance was the owner of everything & nothing. What she owned—possessed—could be carried around in her purse: an embroidery cushion & some blunt needles.

On Emily struggled.

Having never felt the urge myself I can only surmise that your intentions to marry this young man are genuine.

They are, Aunt.

Otho saw fit to cut in with, & may I ask why you are yoking yourself to someone whose extravagant tastes, & extravagant behaviour, our family's resources & our reputation may struggle to accommodate?

We don't care to lose you to a showman.

Is that what is happening? Constance said.

You do understand what I'm saying?

I'm not sure I do, as it happens.

I have good reason to believe he is a person of ill repute.

Constance looked to Grandfather for moral support. None came.

That's quite the allegation, she said.

If you are trying to justify his flamboyance?

I'm not justifying anything, least of all that.

That was the only thing she wanted to say in reply, or could think of. Had it even occurred to her that Oscar may be different? It hadn't occurred to her that he might be anything. One day in the fullness of time she expected them to break every bed in the house. But Constance for the time being felt at a remove from her own sexuality—let alone anyone else's.

They had kissed in the park, for heaven's sake! & he had said many—many!—times since that it had been the sweetest & most important exchange.

& for now whenever she initiated a kiss, Oscar responded & seemed to want to. Constance was thus satisfied in herself that they were people of desires. If there was, as Otho suggested, to be something other than that between them then so be it. It was not anyone else's obstacle to overcome.

I have to make you aware of what people are saying. This world of suggestion would appear to be what you are getting yourself into.

It would appear so, Constance said. & you, Grandfather, what do you say?

His eyes were blue pools. He had on the same look he would use when Constance tried to wash his face. & silence, of course, as thick & bland as an omelette.

She found herself looking at the mantel. The owl that didn't tick.

That settles it, she said. I'm so glad you're happy for me.

Emily seemed so surprised, so confused, that it was as if the conversation hadn't taken place at all. Constance inched off her seat & thanked Grandfather for his time. At the door she saw him squeeze her aunt's hand, & it seemed at least for a moment that what had gone before hadn't been especially unpleasant.

Otho & Emily had gone to the window. But Grandfather sat where he was, staring at her with a patriarch's authority & blankness. Constance smiled back at him & questioned the point of that at all. Was the smile for the sake of her own pride? Only a god would know of what she had to be proud.*

* Had you looked a little closer would you have seen an old man looking back at you with a heartfelt smile of his own?

Grandfather, who had no presence in her life & total control over it, was soon to vanish from the world.

If he had been able to speak he might have said that there was no more for him here, & certainly no more pride. No dignity in spending your days with your lap covered in a rug. Time has taken me, he would have said. I have had more fortune than you, yet I have done more with it. For I have lived a life; have you begun yours? What is it that you have imagined for yourself? A moment here or there of being noticed, a glance from a passing stranger (if that)?*

Her name was being called. Gently down the stairs she went to find Oscar in the kitchen. Cook was making toast for him on the range & was being spoken to of the Great Famine. But being from Buckinghamshire, there wasn't much for her to say in return. Before inventing a reason to leave them to it, Cook pulled up a kitchen chair by the range & indicated that Constance should sit. It was here that they often sat on rainy afternoons, the heat of the stove soothing her in a way that she knew she despised, the comfort always accompanied by a caveat. This was her grandfather's home & Constance had only been invited to live there.

The whole matter of one's nature—it made her quite angry. What questions had they been to ask anyone, let alone someone on the verge of marriage? Extravagance, flamboyance, showmanship—they had all become bywords

---

* Allow me. Was he in fact saying this: I have left the world but you don't have to?

for expressing a sense of difference that didn't, as far as she was concerned, go quite far enough.

Her own kitchen in her own house. There wouldn't have to be a cook, although it was to be assumed that preparing meals was beyond Oscar. But he was a dab hand with the toast. He seemed to know that she would like hers very brown & for it to grow cold before seeing any butter.

I'm to take your fieriness as a good sign? he said.

Some tea got sloshed into a cup & the saucer. It was neither Ireland nor England she wanted gone from. It was here or anywhere that even a single member of the Lloyd or Atkinson family could find themselves.

You'd like the tea in a cup, wouldn't you?

That's not the problem.

Oscar took her cup from her & dipped his toast in it. Some sugar sprinkled on to the wet bread.

You'll take care of me, won't you? she said.

xi

A marriage was not such a big event as to call for blisters. In return for the peace of mind afforded by the prospect of a wedding, & the COMPLETE TRIUMPH in being married off to an apparent* scrounger, Constance was soon fed up from tramping around in service of it.

---

* I suggest we lose the apparent.

She came away feeling filthy & irritable from these excursions—Oscar was in a running negotiation with all the florists of Mayfair—& today she was not long in regretting the decision to walk to Mulberry Terrace.

On any other day she may have sighed it off, but getting there on foot took them past some of the worst of London. There were only so many times you could bat away an outstretched hand. On this occasion, an all-encompassing foul humour would be Constance Lloyd's charitable gift to the world.

Oscar's way of dealing with beggars was to find them all very fascinating. This morning on Sussex Gardens he threw a coin into the air before watching the mad scramble to collect it. There was almost a riot. One child ran into a wall; another fell over a dog, which turned around & bit her.

Making their way towards Marylebone, Oscar was startled by the sight of a young man selling newspapers from a shoeshine stand. The young fellow's eyes & nostrils were glowing red. Before him was a squashed hat & in it a single coin. Oscar began counting out quite a sum in change from his pockets. That he went to great lengths to establish the needs of the young boy was a worry.

For Oscar only ever explained himself when he didn't need to.

Do you have any more change?

Isn't that quite enough? she said.

Oscar removed his hat & poured his coins as well as all the boy's meagre takings into it. Rather than haul him away, she walked on ahead while he got his shoes polished—what else did he want for his money?—& it was hardly at random that she was thinking of her brother.

On any given day Constance would have happily seen Otho fall under a moving cart. & she didn't want to, & wouldn't have been brave enough to, give any more thought to his comments at the house.

The real work would be in keeping going as if she hadn't heard a thing. The real work would be in getting through a wedding without Oscar turning it into an opera. Today's dress fitting was sure to make her feel like a donkey—& it was NOT the most important thing in the world; it was just a dress.

But Mrs Nettleship was known to be the most progressive seamstress in London. Her gestures were said to be gentle & precise & deliberate, & the dress would not be a cage. Constance would be able to breathe.

Rumour had it that it was Oscar who was going to design her wedding dress. & Constance was too much a proponent of gossip to disbelieve in it—except when she was its subject, in which case she had become used to being stared at like a zoo animal & talked about.

If she was not said to be on her way to the dressmakers, for instance, she was on her way back from there, & such were the frequency of her visits that their purpose was said to be Oscar's squabbling with Mrs Nettleship over the colour of the dress.

Saffron, they had all decided.

To this she could only nod politely.

& yet the tattling went on. If Oscar was gone from one day to the next, rather than being considered busy (his speaking tour was taking him to such awful places as Shrewsbury & Scotland), he was meant to be fathering a bastard in every town in Britain & some further afield.

Oscar returned bareheaded to her side, bringing with him an entire bale of newspapers. The young paperboy was departing to gorge himself with his takings.

You have no idea how much of a soft touch you are.

Very much of one, I imagine, he said.

& I understand that you're in love with the world, darling, but why do you want to marry me?

Because I feel incomplete without you.

The statement to which she offered no response came rather too quickly for her liking.

xii

Mrs Nettleship was a barely communicative woman who was either unaware of her fine reputation or in the humour to disprove it. There was a cadre of girls working under her, & she was quick to let them all know whatever they were doing under these oppressive conditions was wrong.

Constance was no one to talk, but the seamstress had a fumbling way of pinning fabric—an ominous-looking muslin tent that was supposedly the beginnings of a wedding dress.

It only mattered what she wore on her wedding day because her family would not be seeing much of her thereafter. Her plan was to endure the wedding before stepping gaily into a carriage, waving cheerio in the manner of a new princess.

She would disappear to very little fuss or complaint.

There was so much muslin that she wondered whether Mrs Nettleship was decided upon mummification. Oscar was hovering, with Constance's sketchbook in hand.

Softer, Mrs Nettleship, don't you think? More carefree.

Constance could hardly speak to register her discomfort. She held her breath, hopefully, for twenty seconds, more.

Look at the drawing like I asked you. It's a garment not a shroud.

Was there something the matter with her drawings? It was not a feat of engineering she was after. But Mrs Nettleship, who may well have resented clients with their own opinions, fussed at the canvas without making any notable adjustments.

Constance repeated herself.

I am a person not a dummy.

That'll do for now, Oscar said.

He was, naturally enough, getting on Mrs Nettleship's nerves. Who's the dressmaker around here? she said.

We'll take over from here.

Mrs Nettleship walked out then. One of her girls was sure to bear the weight of her frustration. & having made a new enemy, Constance found herself left alone with Oscar, who pulled up a chair to absorb himself in pinning the fabric. He was letting the toile fall as freely as Constance had drawn.

It might come as a nasty shock to the world, he said. But I do want to be married.

& all that entails?

This was one question requiring an answer.

Oscar was carrying on like a boy set on threading string through a conker who had then found himself with a crab apple & a coil of rope. She was nevertheless fascinated by his concentration on her dress. & there was a certain thrill in being ignored by someone in the midst of their own struggles.

Perhaps by diverting all his attention to her body he was telling her all she needed to know—wasn't the dress the reason they came here?

We do have a wedding night to contend with, she said.

I intend for us to make the most of it.

Sex isn't everything, Oscar. But it is something.

He made another adjustment & stood back to look at his handiwork. If it was a question of couldn't, he couldn't figure out what he was doing. One by one, he began to remove the pins from the muslin.

I quite agree, he said.

They were starting again with the dress.

& you have desires?

Talk about a funny question.

There was something about being down to her drawers that made her willing to speak so freely.

You do find me worthy of desire?

Oscar turned her so that she saw herself in the mirror. There behind her in the reflection, he was paying close attention to her unadorned trapezius, the palest part of her. In a matter of weeks, she would be naked before him. & wasn't this just how she had wanted to appear? Unable & unwilling to protect herself. The state of undress gave her the very same armour she had been lacking ever since the long afternoon in Lancaster Gate.

& there have been others? Before me?

That sort of thing.

They did of course phrase things carefully. But the words did not seem like their own—if this was as much as Oscar was going to concede, then it was as far as she was going to push him. & it was not as if their conversation corresponded to reality, or if it did the two things were as relative to it as muslin was to satin.

Very well, she said. I won't ask any more about your past. & nor will I expect you to be anything other than who you are. When we marry, there is to be no—All I would ask is that there will be no other woman.

The whole point in being married, after all, was to remove the presence of other people, & other women fell into that category.

Like everyone else, she had had to rely on common gossip for her information on Oscar, who was notorious as much as anything for his romances, certain aspects of which—their spaciousness & frequency—made her queasy. Rumour had it that, in order to get one down from a tree, he would once upon a time have proposed marriage to a cat.

Constance did not really trust herself, but had done all that was possible to disregard the Florence Balcombes of the world, who were by now nothing but phantoms. & wasn't it better for him to have played a little in the field—what field? —than to have to admit to inexperience?*

Mind what I say, he said. Nothing shall stand in the way of our love.

& no one?

Oscar's reaction for once in his life contained a butler's curtness.

She was still standing there in her underwear. The thrill had been fleeting.

This was the problem with imagination—if she could imagine Oscar's skin, & laying herself across the span of his chest, Constance could imagine that same chest draped with Florence's hair as she moved inevitably down, & among other things his curls entangled in hers, the dismal mane draped over his lap, & Oscar spasming minutely to her touch, his hands, defter & more assured than today, removing the silk that would be much like Constance's own, only finer.

With Oscar's eyes not elsewhere but on the blankness of her shoulders, Constance wished herself free from this chemise. & for a moment there came to her the idea of undressing entirely

* Perhaps I felt the same way about you.

& somehow politely joining in on imagined tussles between Oscar & whomever.

That settles it, she said.

For all that was in her mind, & for all that in this very room one thing could have led to another with Oscar, she was not unaware of Mrs Nettleship hovering in the doorway.

Nor did Constance mind that she & Oscar were being regarded as though they were lunatics.*

I would kiss you now if I could, he said.

At your peril.

xiii

Someone was calling out. Constance wanted nothing more than to be unable to hear the voice & her own name being called. & this is what she tried to do, & in one way her wish was granted. When she opened her eyes, she couldn't see a thing.

It was her blessed wedding morning & she was completely unable to see.

& Dolly, sensing something was the matter, sat on the bed & held her hand. She was saying something, & in her tone could be detected concern. She was at pains to explain that one eye was closed over. It was as though a wheelbarrow of red sand had been tipped on it.

---

* Lunatics? Intruders, more likely. On our best days we were both.

That's how it feels, Dolly! Sabotaged by my own body.

Dolly went to the nightstand to run the tap. She returned with a hot facecloth, & the rubbing of it melted the infection in the eye, offering a small amount of respite but without restoring the vision.

A few minutes of facecloth torture before Dolly announced that she looked a little better. But Constance was looking through lace yet, & all she wanted was for it to remain there & to be behind this curtain & to drift back to sleep behind it & remain incapacitated all day & for her entire marriage to come.

Constance let a few moments pass before allowing Dolly to lead her to a mirror, where a gargoyle was to be seen smiling back at her. Her eye a ripe plum that looked soft but wasn't.

Is that me?

It must be, miss.

I shouldn't think I have an understudy at my disposal. So I suppose we should get dressed.

She got the impression that Dolly was merely relieved to be getting on with it. The dress was unsheathed. & Constance soon was doing her best to be without any other thought than of herself in a church about to be wed. Once she had it on, there was no doubt that Mrs Nettleship had in the end known what she was doing.

Running her finger along the myrtle leaves, noting the many hours it must have taken to apply the pearls to her veil, scores of them hardly visible. & ashamed by her own timidness then, Constance opened her palm & took a fine handful of slimy satin.

She was going to wear this dress once & only once, & her hope was that in whatever was to happen today she would not mind herself or her bad eye too much. If the fabric was to end up stained or spoiled, she would not allow herself to become overwhelmed, or irritable or snappy, the thought of which was reason enough to get the beautiful dress on & off as quickly as the occasion would allow.

The satin breathed surprisingly well, &, depending on the way she squinted, the ivory colour was either mysterious or indistinct. Just as she knew she would, she had gone through several moods of her own—all of this stemming from not being able to see, & being frightened by what she could see, as well as trying not to think of why neither her mother nor Aunt Emily had chosen to propose a celebratory breakfast nor send her off in a nice way.

Of course there would be Dolly to help with the girdle & to keep watch over her for the morning. For she was moving around the dressing room with a sense of grace & efficiency that Mrs Nettleship & others could have done with emulating.

To make herself feel better, Constance, with a hand over her eye, said, No one other than Oscar understands that I only want to dress up as me.*

If there were several Oscar Wildes, there were this morning at least two Constances—one who wanted to be lifted up from where she stood & carried head high out of the house &

* If I have my time again, I'll be a butler.

into the church to the accompaniment of trumpets, the other who would have bicycled there in divided skirts. It was safe to assume that Oscar would have been pleased to see either one. For she could not look at herself in the mirror without expecting him to be standing there saying, Nothing shall stand in the way of our love.

Their relationship had progressed enough for Constance to be able to say there was no love like new love. The love of a woman on her wedding morning was something different. Was it this soldiers intuited on the eve of battle? Did the men marching their way to the Transvaal colony experience the same excitement & potential for disgrace?

You're beautiful, miss, Dolly said.

Constance could only laugh.

I am, aren't I?

xiv

Grandfather was so frail that Constance, against her aunt's will, had not only to lead him from the house but to the waiting carriage. She considered looking back with her one good eye as the carriage rattled away, but didn't.

Her wish that she should be free to start a life of her own was being granted. But it was her wish for Grandfather that he would soon be gone from this house forever. Poor Grandfather. But she would rather have drunk pus than spend another night under his roof.

The way they were driving made it feel as though she were already attending a funeral. At least in the few minutes it took to reach the church Grandfather found his way to doze. Constance asked the driver to go once or twice around the block so he would not be disturbed so soon after dropping off.

& could she have joined him, for she had had to struggle her way through so many lunches & so many tributes to the engagement that she felt ready to burst & fit to drop. & this had begun even before the proposal. One day Oscar had taken her, with Otho only too ready to be their escort, to the Great International Fisheries exhibition. The enormous aquarium had inspired a reverie about little girls running along with fishing poles the colour of whose nets matched the bows in their hair. That was all very lovely but the words to her felt like someone else's. & Constance should have hesitated to say so. What happens next? she wondered. Do they all break into a version of 'Ring A Ring O' Roses'?

The daydream was indeed all Oscar's property, for hadn't he lost a sister? & it was for her sake that he wanted to father daughters, & a great many of them. Constance only hoped she would be able to provide, & pointed out that he would be required to play the starring role.

Star isn't the word, said Oscar. Behold the supporting player, he said, enchanted by his own words.

The tanks full of inert fish only brought to mind thoughts of suffocation & entrapment. Afterwards, & to Otho's accustomed disapproval, Oscar had had to calm her with brandy & calmed himself then to the point of passing out.

To prepare to be married was to be weighed down with the morbs—&, often, fury—& listlessness & distraction & doubt. So she would draw a breath, & another, & she would compose herself & would remain composed. She would behave as a bride was supposed to behave.

She was out of the blue assaulted by an image of those coins in the paperboy's hat.

Oscar's debts had, in the weeks leading up to the wedding, needed some attention. Aunt Emily by way of insurance had taken her to see the family firm.

A family of lawyers with its own lawyer—this Constance had found so hilarious she almost peed herself. But her aunt Emily was not much for humour. It was not cruelty but dullness she would use to kill a conversation.

You mean to tell me, she said, that your husband-to-be regards your money, the family's money, our money, someone else's money, as his? & his money, what there is of it, as his?

Sounds like a funny marriage to me, said the lawyer.

& what a riddle it was.

It hadn't helped that Constance had had to explain Oscar's absence on a speaking engagement, & that the payment he received for his work was variable—a word that seemed to so excite everyone that Emily managed to twist it in malicious ways.

Oscar was variable, too, she said. Was it that Grandfather would ever cut her off? was the question.

Not yet, came the answer.*

Grandfather woke up. He seemed to know that they had reached Sussex Gardens. When they left the carriage & climbed the steps to the church, her myrtle wreath was almost swept away by a breeze, the veil lifting to give the gathered parishioners a view of her plum for an eye.

Constance did hope they liked what they saw & that they knew they were looking at the face of modern London. Yes, this was what she had been called.

Constance—ordinary, curious Constance—would not have admitted this at all. She was someone else from somewhere else, &, strictly speaking, wasn't it Oscar they were all waiting for? Around him there was always crowd of onlookers & disbelievers. She hoped they would get what they had come for.

The church was gloomy in the way of home. She could with the one eye not see anyone but Oscar & the flowers over which he had fussed & negotiated & worried.

He was in the modest frock coat they had discussed. The blue coat, & grey trousers & pink tie, was ostentatiously modest, or rather it was the ordinary coat of a man who if he did not understand the purpose of restraint had at least acknowledged the need for it & its balming effect on others, which in its own way was all for show.

---

* No royal wedding, this.

In the way she had gotten herself up, Constance herself had not understood the difference between show & restraint. But she would behave as a bride was supposed to behave.

The blank looks being directed at her said that the eye was something or nothing to be worried about.*

Who else was here, then? The answer was Mama. Although the maternal presence in her life was somewhat theoretical, her mother's presence at the wedding was actual & surprising.

Nowadays Mama slipped in & out of Constance's life without any discernible footprint, unless the magical ability to conjure sinister silences could be called a mark. Mothering was nevertheless an achievement, & no one was more of a mother than on their daughter's wedding day. Mama was thus done up in something elaborate & vampirish. Clever Mama.

With all eyes supposed to be on her, Constance kept watch on her mother. & while she was doing it, guessing as to whom this odd woman was related. & what was Mama doing on Oscar's side of the church? It was as though she was there only to peer at him. Subtly, & not so subtly, with that bare gaze of hers, & no attempt to disguise it, showing a benign distaste for her own kind.

---

* You were dressed memorably & marvellously, my dear, but the occasion was as sober as a vicar's breakfast. I could spy Mama's feathers—it was the poor peacock I was worried about. & no need to see Willie to feel him whispering. Marrying for money was all Mama had ever wanted for her sons. & I could hear Willie's way of putting it. The grandfather's about to croak. Coffers about to open. I was liable at any time to go & cuff him one. Yes, come let us forget this day.

Constance was going to choke. What was worse, no one would have guessed it. There was only one thing for it—she would be better off never speaking to anyone in her family again. It was enough to make her think she should get married more often.

She had been thinking that the very moment in which she & Oscar were pronounced man & wife would be a good moment to demonstrate her true character. Was there supposed to be a kiss? She had hoped there would be. But this had been the one thing on which her darling mother & her aunt Emily had managed to agree. Kissing in church was for common folk. Did the Queen kiss anyone at her wedding? She did not.

This was about as far as Grandfather could go. & LJW evidently thought it was her place to take over. She stepped out from her pew.

I wonder what it is you are like, she said. It's not of this earth.

Constance could only smile at the smooth choreography, as if this were something Grandfather had in private been rehearsing. She was led then to the altar & shown where & how to stand. LJW cuffed her son on the arm to indicate that he should step forward so that the ceremony & Constance's new life could begin—that is, if she had been alive at all, in Lancaster Gate or anywhere.

She heard someone speaking. She thought she would like to listen to what was being said but didn't hear the words. Oscar's feet were moving this way & that. She turned altarwards so as to invite him to reach for her. But there was a feeling of other people there & it was not so easy to breathe. It took her aback, how nervous he was, but the spirit required to survive the occasion had offered him a chorister's grace. Constance had assumed that marriage would bestow upon them both a chorister's purity, for it was now she wondered if someone else had had the best of him.

But she had only to feel her palm in his & that he was taking her hand in a way that said: notice how fiercely I'm holding on. & Constance would not remember ANOTHER THING of this occasion, for she was hardly alive now, & this day was bringing with it a state of mind that resembled a faint & perplexing orgasm, an incoherent feeling of rapture that like everything else in life was passing her by.

xv

LJW was making careful folds in her napkin. It was only fitting that the wedding cake had been too much for the bread knife, which felt suggestive & pathetic in Constance's hand. In the hope that one day she would find this funny, she sent Dolly to fetch another one so that Oscar could cut the cake into bricks before handing them around. The cake's scent was of sherry, which recalled childhood & childhood's anxieties.

A safer bet would have been that Emily had ordered that there be no alcohol at all. Constance had had a lifetime's share of undrinkable tea in this room & had considered often the matter of what to serve at her own wedding. But when it came to it, she was altogether quite vague with impatience. She didn't care what anyone was eating; she knew in her heart that the day was for getting through. For Constance was not surprised, & was even a little amused, that the reception had all the cup-fiddling of a morning at a church hall.*

No one had asked for the pin from her veil. & everyone—Mama, even Otho, whose home this was supposed to be—was standing back against the walls, all attention focussed on their own breathing, as if a net had been thrown over them & had begun to tighten, trapping them all inside while keeping Constance & Oscar on the other side.

With other weddings she had been to, Constance had been alive to the delicacy of the decoration on the cake, & the SHYNESS OF THE BRIDE & the flashes of gallantry from the groom. Better not to consider other weddings in the middle of your own. For this was a gathering with all the vivacity of a queue for meat pies.

Oscar was attempting to talk to Grandfather, who, if it were possible, looked more wretched than he had all day.

What conversation she could overhear was as stilted as the cake was dry as the tea was stewed. Oscar's nostrils were open & he was sucking in his stomach, a sweet, kind self-consciousness to which Constance, like no one else in the room, was susceptible.

But he had been dragged down by the day too.

---

* At least they must have enjoyed watching us suffer.

She had thought she had seen them all by now, but the expression he was using on her grandfather was something like knowingness, except on Oscar this came across as disenchantment, as though there were another wedding reception he must attend & another grandparent in need of his company. He could turn himself on & off like that.

There weren't enough plates for the cake. Not easy, either, to bark orders with an eye like a cricket ball. Constance was glad to escape to change into her going-away outfit: a crimson dress—that matched her eye!—& a wide-brimmed hat that caught Oscar in the nose when he bent to kiss her as she came back into the room.

She teased him for it but he didn't hear.*

Walking as slowly as they could, arm in arm, they did the room once & once again. The blank expressions did not change as Oscar took her hand to begin a dance, their first, one with no music—a very gentle sway like that of a moving carriage, & which was meaningful only to them, & then only just.

Was there any point in performing before such an unappreciative audience? & now they had started they were obliged to keep going a little while longer. If only looking STUPID was all that would be required of her today, for she was looking into her husband's serious & defenceless eyes & it was obvious—quite how Constance didn't know—that something had changed, from the way LJW now chose to

* Had we kissed all day? No, for we had barely even spoken to one another. & you wore your wedding dress for the sum total of two hours & fifteen minutes.

address her as Mrs Wilde to the way she had had to lead Oscar around the room & for how long they held each other's gaze before he looked away.

Whispering, he said, If we slip away now we'll make the three thirty at Charing Cross. Dover before nightfall.

They stumbled & were the only ones to find it funny. She wished for a moment that they had gone all the way. Falling over might have caused more of a stir.

What is everyone looking at?

They're expecting a speech, she said.

I haven't prepared anything.

Grandfather stayed up especially.

A nap might have been more worth his while.

She could see Oscar was trying to find the words. The dance had failed to elicit much of a reaction & he was gambling, she knew, on the right kind of delivery. But the hand that held hers was trembling.

When it came to public speaking, the fact remained that the guise of seeming well had very little to do with how a person truly was. It was keeping quiet that was important, keeping in control of the normal worries & black fears which, as they would THREATEN TO OVERWHELM, you gulped back into yourself.

That was her measure of a person, their willingness to remain quiet. If you had to go around telling people all about yourself—well, good for you.

He was most adept in talking to strangers, & many was the passing acquaintance that considered himself to be close friends with The Oscar Wilde. But this was not a public engagement—this was her family, & his.

In real life Oscar would shock you with his reticence, nay, his inarticulacy. He was a man of words—everyone said he was—but not, they said, of any great sincerity. This misgiving was as much part of their relationship as was a family member. She had felt it at James's Hall & at Park Street & at Ely Place & in Hyde Park, at Mrs Nettleship's, & it would travel with them into their marriage, & lie there, most likely, in their marriage bed. If it would one day disappear she would probably miss it. She would want it back.

Oscar began to speak.

Any more than I can name my current emotions, my feelings for Constance are not material for an oration to beloved mamas & grandpas. It belongs to me only to say that she looks perfect. There is nothing else I can say that will add to or take away from her beauty, & my worthlessness before it. I would only make a fool of myself.

LJW was not saying a word. But she was dabbing her eyes, & Aunt Emily's features had softened from outrage to confusion. For the first time in her life, Oscar's existence in the room may not only have been acknowledged but appreciated. It would be a long time before Constance would understand her aunt. She would be just as old, with the same wariness in the eyes & perhaps as weak under the chin & as easy to disregard.

Yet Constance felt the urge to ignore the blessings at hand & cast aside the potential for any deep feeling in the mad dash to that point in your life where you felt nothing at all.

Oscar, as if he had been all of a sudden transformed into a hunting dog, began sniffing the air.

She was near lifted off her feet then, before being whisked out as though she were being ejected from her own house. Constance had to hold a scream at bay. Was this part of the plan or had Oscar been seized by the moment? She decided it was impetuousness, just as it was impetuous for her to kiss him there in the hall, taking care not to bite through his lip.*

Everyone can see you, came a familiar voice.

Even through the wall, LJW's eyes were fixed on them.

xvi

For a good couple of miles, until they were passing along St James's, she was unable to believe that they were ON THEIR WAY. She kept on looking back & at Oscar, who remained quite still &, not for the first time today, was perfectly unreadable.

Splendid, was it not, to see our families in one room?

The better to see what we're running from, she said.

To, my darling. We're running to.

The carriage was so loaded with their luggage that it was crawling along, but the road running under them was all she had pictured, a future & the journey into it just beginning.

---

* Only later would we come to understand that this was another part of the performance.

After weeks & years of imagining this scene, it was finally & irrefutably upon them.

Oscar tapped her arm. He took some cake from his coat pocket, holding it up to the light as though he were a geologist examining a fossil. Indeed, the cake did resemble a small rock. He had probably secreted it away for her amusement, evidently assuming stale cake contained some kind of REASSURANCE.

To return the favour, she popped some into her mouth.

Cheerful was as cheerful did.

For she was sure she had it all wrong. She had been told, by LJW & others, what it was you were supposed to look for in a husband. Uprightness & nobility & stoicism & physical strength being the vital components of masculinity. Would these be the characteristics found in someone such as Oscar, who was opposed to any normal conventions? In this he was very sincere. Perhaps it was Constance's own sincerity that should have been under question, & perhaps Oscar had already been doing so, & was the one making allowances for her?

Do you think we'll make the three thirty?

Dover train isn't until five.

xvii

Was THE WHOLE OF FRANCE pleased to see Oscar? Not only did the porter on the train seem to know they had been recently wed, but he wished them well on it.

They understand me here.

Nor was it enough to be recognised. No sooner had he set foot on the platform at Calais than he began addressing strangers on the WONDERS OF MARRIAGE, choosing to ignore the ordeal in which they had participated in favour of all heightened joys & the special status that would now be theirs.*

Constance had no problem with either status or joy. & wasn't it the highest form of contrariness to go into her shell just as Oscar was coming out of his?

While she was familiar with couples carrying on as if a wedding were a pleasant morning in church, it was not possible to regard her own as anything less than a RAVINE that had been crossed on hands & knees. For months they had been unable for even the simplest of intimate conversations, especially with the lawyers, & all the other kinds of negotiations about peonies, late into the night sometimes. & all those visits to Mrs Nettleship for a dress she would wear for A SINGLE MORNING OF HER LIFE.

& the honeymoon plans, there had been many, to which she could now apply herself—what they would do with themselves in Paris, with whom & where, obligatory visits to the opera & to salons, & more dinners with friends & how these would be different to the meals before the wedding, which had taken so much out of her. For Oscar had needed some persuasion by the Hôtel Wagram. Constance was hoping to cure him of his aversion to modest accommodations &,

* You did not know what I was feeling, & you never would.

if they had to send apologies for the odd lunch or dinner, wouldn't they have the perfect excuse?

But even the railway men of Calais seemed to know they were newly married. After the mayhem of Gare du Nord, they had an easier time on the way to the hotel, although Oscar, with all the loose energy of a bouncing ball-bearing, asked for the roof of the carriage to be taken down. Constance heard him—for perhaps the hundredth time—calling out to passers-by, & the blissful, boiling afternoon, that he was the luckiest man in all of Paris.

Wasn't this all a bit much? But when was he ever predictable? In that moment, she loved him for it.*

Naturally she had been giving some thought to their plans for the evening. LJW had had a few words to say on keeping Oscar stimulated. Something spicy, like a good mulligatawny soup, to which could be added a raw egg or three. Stimulating drinks had to be encouraged, too. In Paris, there was to be no shortage of those.

As they turned onto Rue de Rivoli, one friendly faced but obviously stupid-looking gendarme was called over to be asked not for directions but whether in fact he was married. It was Oscar's sincere advice that something as flimsy as a vow, & as casual as signing your name on a piece of parchment, guaranteed freedom & invisibility for any reprobate. Free passage for life in the disguise of a respectable man.

---

* Did it never cross your mind that I was putting it on?

Oh my, she thought. Have you been battered senseless by emotion? What a way to speak to a policeman.*

The gendarme regarded them warily & gave no indication as to his marital status.

Something other than marriage had to be contributing to Oscar's mood: the leaving of England, the mirage of a few weeks abroad & some exposure to an altogether different & delectable kind of riffraff. Or was it the simple prospect of a bath, & whatever else, when they reached the hotel?

Rather than QUESTION how such an exultant humour had come about, or speculate how long it might last, Constance, for the sake of playing the dutiful wife, became artificially—yet aptly—extrovert.

The urge to explain may have been a contagion from Oscar, or it may have been travelling from far inside, or merely from the mammalian part of her brain. Or it may have been altogether sourceless. & with the carriage pulling up before Hôtel Wagram, abruptly, as if she had been stung by a bee, Constance stood up in order to cry, No grandfathers!

Standing up & shouting at the top of her lungs had not been part of the plan. In the unlikely event that Aunt Emily were to happen past, she would have been APPALLED.

All the better to scream then, No aunts, no brothers.

No mothers! was Oscar's call.

---

* Were those my exact words? Are you sure you're not overstating it?

They were a match all right, & a match for this city. Paris, the home of love & the home of this new love affair between forethought & recklessness.

No mothers! went the duet.

& there was Oscar, standing on the pavement, with a hand outstretched to lead her from the carriage. He too was taken aback by her outburst.

xviii

It was a suite of three small rooms &, much like Dolly's quarters at home, not modest or immodest but dirty, & dirtier than she had thought France would be. The sweaty BOY carrying their trunks didn't like his place of work any more than they did. The lad was panting too theatrically for her liking, & didn't get on with the unpacking until he was reminded. It was left up to Constance herself to pull the curtains.

Something was off-smelling. A stew of dead flowers, or worse.

Oscar made a show of pacing the floorboards in the sitting room & sniffing the air, which she found amusing until the boy traced the sod smell to a something hiding in a sideboard drawer. The entire drawer was removed with great speed.

The poor animal mustn't have felt a thing, Oscar said.

The porter returned, & with the windows opened no more was to be said about it.

City cries came in then, & something all the way inside

Constance grew colder, all the way down—not on account of the fresh air but from the way in which the porter was stacking Oscar's books with a wordless altar-boy grace. A buck-toothed mouth that was too large for his face, a nose too long & wide, its alpine slope, & she had to double-check that there were ears under all that greasy hair.

There was nothing other than English coins for a tip, & Oscar tried instead to offer a spare copy of Pater's *Studies in the History of the Renaissance*. The boy said he wasn't much of a reader & asked if they couldn't give him some money later; he did not seem to mind when.

His little voice was strange and song-like, as though a furry animal had been taught language. There was no harm in agreeing to see him later, at which the boy left & returned brandishing a decanter of brandy & a plate with a few biscuits sliding off it.

Constance was against him hanging around. But Oscar was so intent on talking about the beauty of Canterbury cathedral, & the boy was waiting until he was finished before he could go.

Every nod, every blink, Oscar took as a sign to go on about the exquisite ordinariness of the brown damask wallpaper. In response to the continued questioning—if he wasn't a reader, what then was he?—the boy could only shake his head, half in shame & half in boredom. Eventually, she hoped, Oscar would pose a question the poor fellow could answer. 'Would you be in a position to find the source of the Nile?'

One accidental & endearing consequence of this exchange, in which the boy's contribution was to remain angelically mute, was Oscar's quest for dominance in a conversation about books.* On she listened, willing him to be quiet, for another twenty minutes, more. Even with a young foreigner, he would have had himself feared as well as admired.

It bothered Constance that she had to speak out at all, & there was exasperation in her voice when she interrupted to say she was tired & wished to sleep.

Oscar's oration came to a halt & he bowed. But the boy, as he was turning to leave, found himself the recipient of an unexpected kind of gratuity.

Oscar had gone to one of the trunks & from it removed his American fur coat. He was draping it now over the boy's shoulders. The boy looked at the coat with a half-smile, buck teeth biting his fat lip. The fabric on the sleeve, as if he would be doing Oscar a favour by taking it away.

Constance wondered if he wouldn't have been more impressed by a box in the side of the head.

It's as if it was MADE for you, Oscar said.

Constance pictured him sleeping under the coat, or having it sold within the hour. Which was likely Oscar's intention.

She was going to ignore this; she was going to try. For she did not really care. Whereas Oscar looked disarmed &, she could well imagine, instantly rueful. Neither he nor the boy knew what to do next. & neither Constance nor the boy thought he suited the coat. He was swamped by the collar alone.

---

* It needn't always have been about books.

But how inevitable, & somehow sustaining, the moment seemed to her—not the wastefulness, in which she was well versed, nor that Oscar should go so far in compensating for such desultory service, which was both unreasonable & reasonable, but his time-worn & fundamental need to be loved by strangers. He needed A PAYING AUDIENCE.*

The boy left with a mumbled thank you, not before Oscar grabbed his arm. He was expected to return later, for further payment.

Have coats to spare, do we? Constance said. Nothing but the best, is that it?

If only he had answered she would have taunted him further. Instead, she took to the bed in a hot & silent fury, listening to Oscar swig from the decanter, & the bedsprings as he sat to undo his boots, & sigh, & wonder if there was any more where that brandy had come from.

An hour or two later, once she had slept, she woke to see him placing her coat on the last remaining hanger. As she lay dozing, she felt herself smiling at the fastidious way in which he picked off imaginary lint, before bowing in imitation of the long-departed porter.

Oscar was the one who had been so silly about the coat, so it was not really for her to continue. & yet.**

---

* You did not know, & I would not have told you, that my reason for offloading the silly coat, which I had considered not packing at all, had nothing to do with the dumb boy & everything to do with impressing you. Should I have done nothing? But how does one do nothing?

** Nothing would have happened otherwise.

Will that be all? she said.

I can't very well open any more windows.

Aren't you forgetting something?

Oscar perched on the very edge of the bed. His bottom lip she could see was quivering.

As far as I'm concerned we're both as virginal as these pillowcases.

Speak for yourself, my darling, he said. Those pillowcases have seen better days.

You can tell me everything.

Syphilis, insanity, depravity.

Quite the list of accomplishments.

It was best to make these little jokes, was it not? The week before the wedding, LJW had invited her for dank tea in a darkened room &, if it were possible to be both cryptic & overly direct, had spoken at length about syphilis & the absence of a cure for it. Constance supposed there would be sores, but they weren't the half of it—the body rot & then the brain. Gonorrhoea was much easier to live with, she was glad to hear, although it did make you introspective. & there was quite enough introspection in her life.

Shall I go on? he said in his most even-handed tone.

There's nothing wrong with you.

Did I mention stage fright?

Something about the look on his face, the fear & sincerity, made her want to be polite.

May we kiss?

Oh, be my guest.

His head lurched towards hers.*

As soon as they were kissing—were you supposed to feel it begin?—she was in herself A RAVENOUS GULL.

When it came to it, that was her kissing personality & Constance was choking as much of him as she could fit into a single mouthful. She wanted to consume him a hundred times over.

The insides of his lips were as tender as, or tenderer than, lamb's liver. As though her appetite alone could sustain them & nutrients were to be drawn from his saliva, she sucked & sucked at him.

& she stopped.

For her mouth muscles had grown tired &/or too much was occurring to her—was he breathing through his nose?—& her wish was not to be conscious at all, for there to be no access to words

But there was the rhythm of her heart & HER HEART AT REST.

& Oscar? Was she to give him up for dead?

If he was anywhere, he did not appear to be in his body anymore.** There he was, moving on & off the bed so fast that he was creating currents in the air.

& now he was naked.

Had they shaved a bear & then cast it in candle wax?

She had a very good view of it. If his mouth had seemed

* It was in my mind the smoothest of gestures.

** I'll bloody well tell you where I was. I was as much there with you as you were there with me.

so precious & liver-y, his penis at that angle was a wooden tent peg overlaid with a child's skin. & it was waving about, which, she supposed, was reason enough to get on with it. Before everything went on the retreat. There was no doubt that it would.

But it had never occurred to her that she would in her marriage bed need help undressing. Where was Dolly now? Oscar pulled everything off her in such a way that she knew he was familiar with female undergarments. The breeze was caressing her bareness, & for a brief moment she wished the windows she had wanted open could be closed.

& she thought then of the drawer that been removed & what had been in it.

He didn't like it when she licked his nipple.

He didn't like it when she took him in her hand.

Her inner workings were not quite there either. & she was startled that he spat on his palm & rubbed himself so that all very cordially he could—the bruiser—get his way into her.

He pulled a face. & Constance was surprised & then not surprised by the matter-of-fact-ness of a wince.

She thought of saying something.

Are you enjoying yourself? You don't seem to be.

But it delighted her that he would put himself through something he didn't enjoy just to please her. How could he bring himself to do something he hated? So many delights in one day. This was how she knew he loved her.

She could hear his breathing, which meant he could hear hers, the trepidation she was carrying.

Now he was counting.

One for every thrust—one two three four five six seven eight nine ten—&, as she was waiting for him to reach a certain number before they could declare this a success, she felt this lump of a man tremble.

& thus she assumed it was all working & with a SHUDDER then it was working too well & he was back to counting. A brute with a solid appreciation of arithmetic.

Oscar had a job to do, as did she. Hers as far as she could tell was to lie there & make him aware of her ongoing pleasure. She was willing herself towards orgasm, for without one she was told no child would form in her womb. All this for the continuation of the species in which Constance herself had very little faith.

They reached zero then.*

* I tried at first to conjure music, something triumphant, but nothing I heard I was able to recognise, & this made me immediately sad. A few more thoughts petered out before I was able to fix on one image to get me through. The buck-toothed boy was hopping & skipping around before me. My gaze for a while moved around the scene, from floor to ceiling, the window to the door, but the boy, golden & bright, was the vital component of it. It was the same as when I masturbated. I could furnish all the rooms I wanted, but I couldn't get the people in it to do anything interesting. Nobody ever moved; I had for myself a nice collection of wooden puppets. So often was I let down by my own fantasies. At least here the boy had the gumption to move about. & then I thought, whatever can I ask the poor chap to do? Being ill at ease in a fantasy was part of the fantasy. I felt gloomy for a moment. & didn't the boy choose this moment to pull a surprise? A puppet without any strings, he began to slide across the bedroom floor. Up onto the bed with him then. Was my gaze supposed to slither after him? But the confusion was exciting & I stayed with it, & the boy, a good servant after all, insisted on

& even though he was still inside her & was pulling out, which was much more straightforward than getting himself in, she was thinking of the next time & how it would be better.

This now was a room in which they had had sex.

Empty head, at least. Inside her were his pearls, the magical trace. Not magical at all but tepid. The evidence.

Afterwards, Oscar wrapped himself in a bed sheet, the one on which she had bled, & went to look out the window. He said he was fine, he just wanted to look outside. In so far as she was still interested in the subject, he was able to come across as entirely rampant as well as entirely sexless.

He was whistling, as though AT A LOOSE END. She could hate him for being so merry, or was it aimlessness? They were not the same thing. She would have to be resigned to them not being.

She pulled herself up to sit, & with eyes fixed on him, she said, I could get used to this.

That's precisely what you'll have to do.

He could hardly speak, & she could hardly hear.

---

playing his part. He knew just what to do. (I would make damn sure that he was properly recompensed.) Make no mistake about it, he was burying his face in the pillow & was, if I was able to concentrate very hard, able to place himself underneath me, just where you were, except he was being perfectly still & was making no sound. Once he was safely in place, I was able to open my eyes & look at the wallpaper—a scene within the scene—which had no qualities to recommend it other than trying to be something that it wasn't. Chrysanthemums in yellow & white & orange. Sweet & immaculate & naturalistic & glaring in their dullness. Silence followed, the lovely boy in such a hurry to make an exit. & when I looked down there you were, peering upwards with curiosity & love.

My Lord, but you're an enthusiastic lover.

As are you.

Come over here & say that, she said.

He went via the washstand to splash his face with water.

I thought you may have wanted some reassurance on a certain matter.

xix

There were a few excursions, not DISASTROUS but trying.

Oscar, like any good Irishman, couldn't say no to the smallest invitation. The whole purpose of a honeymoon was to show each other off, he said.

More samey Whistlers that simply had to be seen, & John Singer Sargent wanted them round for dinner. Sarah Bernhardt—with whom he said he had had an aborted dalliance, about which Constance decided she didn't, or wouldn't, mind—was on somewhere as Lady Macbeth.

On the matter of other women, she had changed her tune. But it was not easy to be consistent when you had The Oscar Wilde for a husband. & hadn't Constance Lloyd received many callers of her own, with all their copies of Tennyson & Keats, & hadn't they all come & gone?

Oh, how she disliked everything about jealousy, especially her own delusions towards it. The time had come & gone when she would have, out of perversion, hallucinated Oscar partaking in alleyway trembles. He had to be allowed his own things, did he not? The grand cafés where he could muffle himself with brandy & where he was known to all but the most reserved of waiters, whom he could cheerily greet without fear of being waylaid.

It was no accident that THEIR PARIS had more to do with scintillating remarks about glassware & upholstery. It even had its own fragrance. If Oscar so much as left for a dander, a bouquet of flowers arrived to take his place. Gradually Constance was sinking into a lily-scented stupor.

But every time she returned to their fortress & their room at the Wagram with its indoor fog & loaded fireplaces, she had a premonition of bereavement.

& then CAME THE RAIN & being stuck indoors. There was a curtain of water before the window & a river running along the street outside. The Tuileries last time she looked had become a basin of brown sludge. At first, Oscar would speak about the rain with uncommon enthusiasm & soon enough Constance was herself an expert on weather. As he turned the page in his book, he would coil a lock of her hair around his finger & she would be waiting to uncoil it again. The lovely mysteries of love. Souls loosely knit. The heart not questioning but longing for the uncertainty that the smarter part of her shunned.

There passed hours, & possibly years, in a room of not indefinite orgasms, & one afternoon they were at home there reading. Constance would forevermore wonder if there was someone else she could have married, about whom she could have had NO DOUBT.

It was the doubt she was after, for it was her apprehension about another that would force Constance to put away the unsolvable parts of her own puzzle. Her own dubiousness, as she saw it. Thank you, Mama. Wasn't one supposed to be A DIFFERENT PERSON in marriage? But she was not in any way different. She was so much the same that she felt on the whole worse.

Was it that she feared a person couldn't be flamboyant without being a bit funny sexually? Oscar was probably both.

& the power of being married to both would be that it allowed her to ignore the person she had been turning into; the ongoing equity between solitude & loneliness, between privacy & emptiness, which could only be resolved by yoking herself to one such as Oscar, who had the capacity to occupy twenty-five indeterminate emotional states simultaneously.

&, for all that she was supposed to have been let go by the evil eye, he only had to YAWN IN THE MORNING to make her want to run away with the circus for fear of being herself abandoned.

There had been no upset. So far.

But she had not been allowing in the porter to clear away, & the air in the room felt turned over, as though there would soon be a squabble over who would take the next breath. Oscar's clothing was scattered everywhere—& she began to wonder if she shouldn't invite the boy back so she could give more of it away.

Not for the first time today did she say, Well.

The assumption being she was talking to herself, & she'd done enough of that in her life.

Well, well, well, Oscar replied.

When he wasn't reading he was drinking, & very often he was doing both.

Don't you intend to speak this evening?

He set down his copy of *Le Rouge et Le Noir* & his glass & began slowly to slur to life.

What if I'm not in the mood for talking? he said.

Except to me.

Yes, of course. Except to you.

They were in a period of acclimatisation; this she had known for days. Had they ever had sex in the first place, that was the question. It had been an experience in which she didn't exist at all. The blood & all the other stuff & the clearing up afterwards & the pain.

There was kissing of course, if they remembered.

Sex the second time was so energising—she had never felt the liquid move so fast in her body—that she had assumed it would be something they would take to with great enthusiasm. For all she knew they would be at it day & night, & to an extent that she recalled LJW's words: too much copulation was not only to be cautioned against but feared. The richness of Oscar's semen was not to be diluted.

You enjoyed that, he said, afterwards.

I did, as a matter of fact. But how would you have known? Your eyes were closed.

So much the better if they could arrange their pleasures once a month; the exact timing was to be adjusted to accommodate the monthlies.

They were not the kind of folk who could make a love from whatever came to hand. Were you supposed to show affection in a box at the opera, in your own bathroom, & everywhere in between? In their case, there were too many options. A place like Paris was no place for lovers*. Was she longing for home already? She was longing for routine, if only as an obstruction to desire.

Desire, then. Already hers had turned inwards & was not to be spoken about. Every day thereafter Constance was compelled to seek sex, as well as compelled to avoid it, notionally in favour of a good conversation, perhaps a nice long conversation, any conversation that wasn't about the rain.

Of all the things she'd dreamed it would be, a marriage was supposed to be well-intentioned madness. With only a little exaggeration, she'd imagined tidal waves. But these few days with Oscar had given her something she had never had: peace, & a man paying her the respect of not hanging on her every word.

She found herself alternating between two states: BLISS & boredom. Wasn't bliss where love found its highest expression & where it went to be put down? It was inevitably humiliating to believe in bliss & even more humiliating to

---

* The commencement of married life in a cheap hotel. Is it any wonder where we ended up? You in the pain of exile & I in disgrace.

have experienced it, like the man believing himself able to fly repeatedly jumping off the roof of the same tall building. She could now see that all this bliss & freeing oneself of expectations of it was not A FALL FROM A ROOFTOP but the only logical & desirable outcome. She was being invited to see how Oscar was when he was alone.

He was rosarying to himself.

Whatever can I say that will impress the like of a room full of painters?

Do you have to impress anyone? she said.

She took his notebook &, without thinking that she shouldn't, read from it, thinking & thinking for an alternative to the word showy.

Restraint?

Might be the end of me, Oscar said.

Let's hear it in your voice.

With face creased in concentration & effort, Oscar, the arch-preparer & worrier, began to read aloud.

The only artists I have ever known who are personally beautiful are bad artists. Good artists exist simply in what beauty they make, & consequently are perfectly uninteresting in what they are.

We do know your tendency to overuse beautiful, she said.

The only artists I have ever known who are personally delightful are bad artists.

No amount of listening could make it sound any better.

What you just said, but less of it.

A little more bliss was in order, she decided.

Oscar's absorption in the act of saying the same thing over & again was tacit approval for the removal of his waistcoat & the undoing of his shirt. These were the actions of any loving marriage. Off came the shirt with only a small amount of theatricality, & as swiftly & as carefully & as convincingly as she could she began to pull down his trousers.

xx

If she slept on in the mornings, Oscar would read in bed beside her. She would awaken with his chin on her shoulder, & before he could be waylaid by the brandy & Stendhal they would lie in bed, nose to nose & naked as newborns, one of his hands between her thighs, pulling her closer, the other one framing her cheek before spreading out her hair to catch the sun on the pillow.

They hadn't changed the sheets—she hadn't wanted them to—& his scent on awakening was a delicious combination of yeast & salt, old dough. Sometimes he looked as lonely as a seabird in winter.

In the amount of sleep he had managed would be set the tone for the morning. Their words were always the same.

You first.

No, you, he'd say.

Me first.

If you must.

I love Paris.

Neither do I.

Sometimes he made a fumble for her—with the question 'Shall I interfere with you?'—& sometimes he didn't. Bustling out of bed then, to his morning coat & reading chair which, as far as Constance was concerned, would have to do them for the day. When she felt very FRISKY, she would leave bed with a handstand & Oscar would applaud, before going back to his book.

Black had to be put upon white, he said. Black upon white.

Once in the performance of a handstand she farted, & there was something criminal in the way she couldn't stop laughing. She tried to calm herself by stamping her feet. When she asked Oscar to fart he wouldn't. She begged him to, & with a reply that was rather too sharp he said that he wouldn't dream of it.

After the charade of the coat, the lucky young porter was keeping himself to himself, except, at Oscar's insistence, to change the flowers & to make new deliveries of old books for rereading, towers of them by the bed & the door & at the foot of his chair.

Oscar liked to read a work in the place where it was written. She had no need for ANOTHER defence of Mallarmé—but he was generous enough to make the case for any book that sat in his lap. & he was better off kept busy reading, for they had gone back & forth about the dinner at Sargent's & whether they could get out of it as she wanted them to.

Why bother going out at all? To be out, on the one hand, & afterwards to be happy to be home again on the other.

It was a beautiful evening in the far north of Paris & swallows were darting in & around the skylights.* Sargent was such a show-off, thus it was no surprise that they were expected to eat in a room furnished in the main by in-the-works canvasses. Many of his subjects were dressed more daringly than she was. There was something of that nature about Sargent too, who when he spoke looked into the space between Constance & Oscar.

It's good to see you looking so well & refreshed.

It was becoming common for them to be addressed as one. Were they beginning to see themselves as others saw them? It was really nothing more than getting used to being looked at as though they were twins in a pram. People looked & smiled & moved on.

Granted, they were starting to dress alike. Up to the nines & why not? Now & then it felt like she was peacocking as much as he was, but only now & then. She had never felt anxious in a plumed hat. & old lace was more effective than a suit of armour.

When would she be able to convince herself she was part of the reason they got invited anywhere? She longed for the time, not so long ago, when this wasn't an issue, when she was merely happy to be away from Lancaster Gate. She was beginning to act like the patient who'd been discharged from

* If only one could have been persuaded to fly around inside. The evening could have done with livening up.

hospital & wished herself back there, for the familiarity of the poisonous vapours & the sweet promise of anaesthesia.

Constance gave a smile when she saw the table set for ten. Oscar would be a mite disappointed that there weren't many for dinner. There was—when was there not?—his tiresome young friend Sherard & a few other whatsisname painter-types, but Oscar had been expecting more of an audience (whereas Constance was giving thanks for the quiet room).

When they got to the table, she thought Oscar was about to sweat through his coat. His face seemed to be searching the soup for the courage to speak up with all his prepared delights.

But they might have dined better at a boarding house. Sargent's days of trying to impress anyone were evidently long past. The meal more than any other proved to be a trial of endurance. Oscar didn't touch the fish course, although he never missed a pass of the wine. As for matters visceral, her plate was crowded with innards & beaks imprisoned in jelly. She was sure she saw an eyeball in there & she ate it before it could see anything. She turned to find her wine had been finished by Oscar, who was having it all, hers & everyone's.

The candles on the tables allowed her to examine some preparatory watercolours on a sideboard. With only so much interest in his work, she asked Sargent if he was working on anything interesting. Half-finished as they were, the studies of the woman were proof enough that still life was preferable to the messiness of the real thing; in real life the light was never right. Art was a life where decisions could be made on the basis of loveliness over physical reality.

Life was so very dim. This room was so very dim.

Not many people she knew were worthy of portraiture. But this woman in the picture was haughty in a way that Constance envied. Was this what Sargent saw or had wanted to see? Although the woman's gaze was evasive, it expressed no anxiety. For she was more alive than Constance was, as well as pleased with her own company, & rich & beautiful & unattainable. All things Constance—who didn't like being looked at at the best of times—was not.

When Sargent asked her what she thought, she told him 'Very nice'. An answer he did not appear to care for. & though she could have gone on, about the convincing way he'd rendered the tautness of the woman's upper arms, she chose not to lest she take too much of the light away from Oscar.

He was eating with his fingers & sucking on his bones. Then, tiring of champagne, after his NINTH GLASS OF IT, he began dispensing absinthe to his left & right, all the while making revelations of their bedroom activities—his fanatical delight in the smallest carnal detail: the inside of her nostrils as he bore down on her, the thinness of her nails as they scratched on his back.

He was always doing that—coming over as racy to conceal his true priggishness—& Constance supposed she should be amused her body was so prized as to be worth bragging about. She did wish he had kept a few things to himself, but Sargent seemed so fascinated that she felt more adored than offended.

Whenever she felt herself insulted, Constance implored herself to take whatever it was as a compliment. Wasn't the most popular animal in London Zoo Obaysch the hippo? & all he did was sit back & do very little, happily inviting ridicule.

When her virginity was deemed old news, Oscar & Sherard began once again to debate French republicanism. She stared at her vichyssoise as Sherard got put in his place over a woman's role in the home, & had to gather all her patience when they moved on to the matter of low-heeled shoes, thus ensuring that Constance would tire of her own special subject.

In the end she drank too much as well.

But, in the taking off of his trousers, Sargent had trumped them all. The sparring between Oscar & his chuckaboo had been so boring that their host had had to provide his own entertainment. But there was something malicious about his conduct, as though he didn't care what his guests thought of him. It was a relief at the nether end of the evening when he took himself to the piano.

If anyone's in the mood for music, I might play a little something.

Oscar paused then to ask for a new glass. He wanted to go back into the champagne. Although he was not over-the-top drunk, for he was served well by his large frame & could drink all day & night.

I'm not one bit in the mood for music, he said. So I invite you to go right ahead.

What's your favourite?

As long as there's nothing from *Pirates of Penzance*.

Sargent winked at Constance, & began to sing.

Away, away! My heart's on fire.

She let herself drift into the song, with Oscar draped around her & holding her hand.

I burn, this base deception to repay / This very night my vengeance dire / Shall glut itself in gore. Away, away!

Sargent turned to Oscar, for whom the gathering had been called & the songs were being sung.

Music is superior to painting which is superior to literature. Hence writers must be the most servile creatures on the planet.

It was not too late for Oscar to have glimpsed the opportunity. There was an obstacle before him, & how eagerly he was about to scale it.

I might agree with you, Sargent, he said.

& on he plunged: The only writers I have ever known who are personally delightful are bad writers.

Oscar had on his make-a-speech face & of course she could tell he was going to go on too long. It was enough to make her cry that his next sentence came out entirely back to front. How well he knew those words, & how she wished he were at the hotel, saying them to himself. But what she wanted more than anything was for him to impress Sargent. & this was not happening in the way that he had hoped for.

Would you do us all a favour, Wilde? Sargent said.

With pleasure.

Please stop talking.

Oscar looked exhausted, a dejection that had he been able to see it for himself would have been the cause of much embarrassment. With some apprehension she found herself whispering in his ear, & regretting it.

Sargent noticed of course, & asked, Do you always let your wife advise you?

Only in the bedroom, Oscar with closed lids said. & she tells me the delivery was better earlier.

How fascinating, Sargent said.

But Constance knew Sargent was the sort to whom nothing was ever truly fascinating, & she knew, in the mercurial way of any artist, that whatever fascination there was would soon turn to boredom & pity.

& she fleetingly felt that pity herself. For she hoped she wouldn't see her husband topple into a canvas in front of all these people. & were he to keel over, wouldn't everyone say that they knew him well? But had they seen him stepping pink & pudgy from the bath into the same underpants as he had been wearing all week? Had they ever witnessed him weeping not over some gesture made in oils but over his sister dead & cold in the ground?

She imagined Oscar rehearsing all over again, & this time getting it right. The DEMON in him thought he did too.

His demons, she thought it as well to list them.

His demons were the coal that burned in the fire that boiled the kettle that heated the water that diluted the absinthe that made him mad. They were the borrowed money to pay for dinners with hangers-on. They were the dashing coat with the unusual collar. They were loose change & polished shoes & a bale of yesterday's papers. They were pretty sonnets for her grandfather. They were tea from a saucer & someone to butter Constance's toast.* They were the proposal that had dried in his throat & the ruby heart held in golden hands. They were the handful of ivory satin. They were hiding up a tree, the famous wit & the less famous shyness.

They were mornings, & soft hands in the straw of her hair, a disembodied voice apologising for having had all of her in one go, leaving her altogether calmer & for dead.**

---

* More demons! More, more, more!

** I'll talk to you about demons, shall I? & where they might take you. It had been, you said, a very educational evening. & you did seem relieved to be home. & perhaps you had lost the will, but you didn't mind that Sherard was waiting for me downstairs. & I'll have you know Château Rouge was his idea. On the double, he said. That was just it. My challenge for the night—& the next, & the next—was to defy the urge to play truant. After a tramp down a medieval alley there was a salon that sported a painted mural mimicking the scene before it: a collection of thieves & ruffians & pimps, all together emitting a ferocious noise. All that was missing was a lion tamer & a sword swallower. Behind the bar stood the proprietor, a cheery ogre with a cosh. One look at us & we were beckoned to follow him upstairs to a room where they had taken the fashion for low lighting a little far. It took my eyes a few moments to register that the shadows moving in the crimson light were in fact bodies. This was the famous morgue. Sherard let out a shiver of disgust, as I'm sure will you when you hear this. But that is the point of telling it. So you know. Truly devoted husbands tended to be tucked up in bed at this hour, did they not? In one corner some young men in wrestling attire were lifting primitive weights. I can't deny that my gaze moved from torso to torso, the angelic bodies & hard faces. You're either married or you're not, I said to Sherard. I told him I wanted him to know how happy I was to be married. A very convincing account of it, he said. One face, North African, stared out at me, &, moving the story along, I accepted his invitation to join him in a room furnished with little more than a Turkish toilet & a bucket. There was a wooden bench too, & I sat on it while my friend undid the buttons on my boots. In trying not to reveal my

After dinner there was a general herding towards the door. Oscar had crawled out of his trough of despair, but twice she heard him say to Sargent & anyone who would listen that they should all repair to the Château Rouge. But they had all had enough of him by now.

xxi

Earlier she had asked for someone to clear away. The bedroom now was just as it was when they had left it. It was beginning to smell like a lakeshore.

Constance was tired but she did not get into bed, for she was frightened of being in it alone. & even though she was gaunt with exhaustion she chose instead to doze in the chair & when she couldn't sleep there she began to masturbate. She had no reason to do so sitting up but did not want to do it in bed for fear of goriness on the sheets. For what seemed an age, & trying to summon up appetising thoughts in a muggy room, she played with herself while fidgeting in the seat.

The lighting was wrong. Too low was spooky but anything more bright & she felt LOOKED AT. She brought the candle

---

fears too much I asked him if he read. But one look at his matted hair & the filth caked into him answered my question. His dirty fingers started then on my tie, but I informed him that I'd be keeping my things on. Do you know, I said, I don't think there's a full evening's work for you in this. I took some comfort in the fact that the poor fellow didn't quite follow me. I undid a couple of trinkets from my wrist & handed them over. His ship had come in, & a night off into the bargain.

closer. The wavering flame was calming & contributed to the sensation of this not quite happening. The scene was set then & featured the skin & smell & decisiveness of a handsome stranger, but more important than fantasy was to avoid the words of LJW & all the arrows she had fired by way of good advice.

The sound of the springs as Constance climbed into bed was akin to applause. She kept going for nigh on an hour until her mouth begin to slacken in a way that foretold peace. But the bangles on her wrist were clinking & she was growing distracted. Oscar could at any moment pile in on top of her, an image which brought with it another line of enquiry: she couldn't help herself imagining the fine welcome she would offer him, & his soft bulk kneeling before her in the darkness.

She thought that she heard someone coming but nobody came. She did sleep but not very well, for she was scared of absinthe nightmares. & when she awoke the room was empty & silent except for the softness of a building talking to itself, that feeling of the walls sinking into the floors. She believed for just a moment that she was having a vision of his mother & hers strapped to the mast of an abandoned ship. The ship was creaking in a storm, & she was content for a while to imagine the storm gathering force & the ship capsizing & taking everyone on board with it.

The darkness was denser for his absence. Oscar had to have his liberty, which was to say she wanted him to have it. & she was happy now to have the bed to herself. It was a little before dawn when she stopped listening out for him.

The Prettiest House in London

i

When Grandfather died not long after the wedding her sense of dread halved & their income doubled.

THANK *YOU*, Mister Death.

A month was plenty of time for her & Oscar to become the strangers they had never had the courage to be. They rubbed along like little boys new to boarding school. Lodgings were found in his old rooms on Charles Street, for the new house was uninhabitable & Oscar was fretting over the smallest details—there was enough correspondence going back & forth on the dining room shelving to fill a Viking longboat—while seeing his way to making a merry hames of the organising. No builders would show up, or else they would be coming & going like ladies of the night. More often than not looking for money for work they hadn't done.

It was becoming safe to assume that she—Mrs Oscar—would on a daily basis receive a note of account from a tradesman with whom he had a complaint & that it would be down to her to both placate her man & cadge about for the funds to pay his bills.

At least Oscar made a very good cup of tea. The making of tea was a sign that he was in good form. She was at her happiest first thing in the morning, when he would be lickety-split on his way to the scullery, before standing before her, legs akimbo, with a tray of tea which was always like the soup left over from a goulash.

This morning he hastened to kick yesterday's things into a corner & a show was made of leaving the shutters flapping. She was preparing to let him have at it, when she noticed that his top teeth were sticking out, presumably in imitation of the porter at the Wagram. Occasionally he would outstretch his hand in expectation of A TIP.

He performed this skit so well that she had to get out of bed to fix the shutters as well as pour her own tea. The staring at the floor came next, & then the centrepiece of Oscar's little performance: the proclamation that the boy couldn't read. Such cruel & delicious mockery.

She could hardly remember the boy anyway. & there was no reason to dwell on the patchy pleasures of Paris, for London was providing the distraction she never thought it would. She was in fact so full of love that she was beginning to tire of the very idea of it.

Oscar's face in the morning, the skin tender & warm, & in his expression a kind of grief that rather than want to assuage she knew to leave well alone. Oh, she had no business knowing who was peopling his dreams, let alone what violence they were enacting on his soul. Picturing instead an unexpected tableau—the French boy singing, say—& travelling ever onwards towards hopefulness and peace of mind.

Nor did she ever want to ask Oscar to clear up properly. It was important to be his wife & not his mother or his maid.* & she could not seem to help abetting him in his quest to spend all his money & hers & more. He would open bills & smile before setting them in a drawer never to be seen again. The appointment of the architect was welcome news, & Constance too put all her weight into seeing that they would have somewhere to live before the turn of the century.

Although they had nowhere to dry their towels, they were, he said, the luckiest people they knew. The finest decorator in London was at work in their house, which would be ready when it was ready, for the space had to be reorganised, rebuilt, redecorated before they could even consider a scrap of furniture, none of which would come cheap, not if it was going to be their own little theatre.

For here Mr & Mrs Oscar would be both at home & on display. In the dining room, white everything was the plan, a little gold &/or pink if she was lucky.

Not knowing the state of affairs, neither how little money they had nor how loath she was to spend it on painting the ceiling, the decorator did not stint when it came to painted ceilings. Faced with a choice between just enough & too much, Oscar would always ask for both. She had never before

* You were, without knowing it, all three.

seen so many lanterns as there were in his library, plus divans enough to offer an entire regiment an afternoon nap.

That Oscar's tastes were excessive but ridiculous struck her as further evidence of his restless brain. & how was it that he had yet to get any of this onto a page? Perhaps a finished house, & a lovely one at that, would settle his brain. & there she was losing all sense of herself in trying to please this stranger, with no idea of how to please anyone who was so busy pleasing himself.

What a terrible beast was pleasure anyway.

& THEY BEGAN TO FIND THEIR WAY. As they snuggled close by the fire, the soothing hand was known to wander into the hollow. But the dark forest in her soul was equal to any loving touch.

At least the tea would appear in the usual way, the eggs boiled past the point where they tried to escape the pan themselves. But she would eat them, smiling. They were very unpleasant to eat & she took great pleasure in doing so. She was happy for Oscar to set out the tray; she marvelled at the perfect egg cup, the addition of a tomato or a slice of cheese. She had always liked cheese on her eggs. Stinkyeggs, she called them.

Their eyes met over spoonfuls of chalky yolk. If only they could have made a life out of such a few morsels, for a meal meant a great deal more than half an hour spent at the table. Any longer than that & Oscar would get bored & she would get embarrassed, as if they were lodgers in the house of a far-off aunt, speaking no more than manners required.

Well, LET THEM be bored & embarrassed, for this was only the stirring of a newness—companionship, praise God for that. It was that which would save them. Dress it up how she wanted, in egg cups & tea cosies, it was comfort which would save them. Sometimes she surprised him with biscuits with the tea.

ii

Today LJW was to be ushered into Tite Street for an inspection; rather, she was coming to see—cast her eye over—how the renovations were coming along.

What she was coming to inspect would amount to a hanging mist of ash-white dust & an abyss seen through a hole in the dining room floorboards.

PROGRESS!

There was now a plank crossing the hole, & a workman performing the circus trick of crossing it with a wheelbarrow. Constance was quick to hop out of harm's way while the fellow was engaged by Oscar on the subject of the shelves in the dining room.

He had decided that lecturing on the subject of decorating qualified him as a carpenter. Assuming that they all spoke the same language, he stood in his velvet coat in the middle of a building site, describing the shelves & how they could be built in & that he was expecting his instructions to be followed to a T.

But NOTHING WAS BEING DONE. & LJW was on her way.

Oscar's eagerness to subject himself to his mother's approbation offered Constance an injection of wilfulness: namely, to be as strident as she could allow herself to be while making it perfectly clear she was seeking nobody's good favours.

Can't we just show your mother the drawings? Constance said.

That would still involve seeing her, darling.

A hole had been hammered through a dining room wall, creating something of a porthole through which to observe the makings of the library, where the painter had begun on the ceiling, a large portion of which was in gold, the rest in yellow & a resplendent slice of pink. This looked deliberate & all wrong.

Oscar had lots to say on the matter of other people's work. Constance had nothing to say except to state that one opinion was enough for any marriage, which was ENOUGH opinions for one day & was on account of LJW, who when she got here would not hesitate to add hers & to ensure they were in opposition to anyone else's. It was impossible to ever know if the woman was being helpful or plain vicious.

Once they're finished whatever damage they are causing, I've asked the decorator to speak with the illustrator at their earliest opportunity.

Constance found herself with a mouth full of cobweb. Oscar cleaned her mouth with forefinger & thumb.

She kissed his fingertips, saying, Are you turning our house beautiful into a little book?

If they're going to paint directly on the walls, I'd like them to know what kind of silk is being used.

Oscar considered her pernickety about money. She didn't want to nag but how else could you make your point? & nor had she made her point. One of these days she was going to have to be more direct.

How much silk were you thinking? she said.

He gestured. The entire bloody room.

About that much.*

How much money do you think we have, darling?

I have had quite an amount. In my time.

Had is not any good. We shall have to work on that. The getting of money & the hanging on to it.

iii

His mother was greeted with a rehearsed chorus of 'Welcome to the prettiest house in London'.

It was not a house Constance would have imagined decorating for herself, not that she would ever have imagined completing a job like that alone.

The hallway was in grey & white & the most delicate & restrained of yellows, but in every other direction there was a new tableau on which the eye could gorge. The dining room had been completed with a carpet that would have induced

* You were, were you not, imagining me with a severed head?

seasickness, the curtains were woven with silk, the notes in the embroidery rhyming with cups rhyming with the tassels on the napkins.

The impression being given was this—the room was just as important as what would happen in it.

& that wasn't even HALF of the downstairs.

Sure enough, LJW walked past them into the library where Oscar explained that within the next week, or few months, they were going to be taken over by Arabs. Gone would be the Morris wallpaper but not the carpets & if they could decide on a suitable author there would be an inscription above the door.*

In this room Oscar was going to deal with his correspondence & his diary, after which he would take the odd nap, keep up with his reading &, when the mood took him, do some writing.

He was referring to their house as an extension of their personalities & Constance was terrified at the thought of living in an extrovert house with a chatty interior, a daylong reminder that she didn't have enough to say for herself. & since Oscar was proposing placing his own portrait next to one of Augustus Caesar, this was going to be a house that would say anything it wanted.

LJW absorbed Oscar's proposal & said, Have you managed to curb his spending, dear?

---

* Finding someone suitable would be a life's work.

Constance looked at the floor. That morning for the hallway he had ordered an engraving of Apollo & the Muses.

One of you should get a job. It can't be you, Oscar, of course.

In these words could be heard the concern of a mother as well as the herald of a challenge. The message was: Oscar was unable to look after anyone, & would need to be looked after.

Constance had to be careful in what she said next.

Would you like the tour?

LJW showed little interest in the speech Oscar had ready for the drawing room. Constance followed her up the stairs to the bedrooms, only a little distracted by a delicious fantasy of her mother-in-law lying at the bottom of the stairs after an unfortunate slip on the carpet.

LJW was about to speak, for nobody else would.

You will give me a granddaughter?

We'll do our best, Oscar said.

Should that any daughter inherit her proportions & not yours. Show him the way, won't you, dear?

I'll do my best, Constance said.

Oscar was looking at her with a kind of pleading. His eyes were enshrouded in mist, which she understood to be related to his sister, a grief he could not communicate in any other way.

LJW went on.

It goes without saying that being in love is possibly the best love. But parenting is akin to being mugged with a hammer.

When Constance walked into the bedroom, her foot became trapped in a hole in the floorboards, & while Oscar bent to release her she returned to the notion of his mother lying at the foot of the stairs. To THAT she added the image of her & Oscar in this very room with the fissures in the wall papered over & them lolling on a divan while he played with her hair & jotted in his notebook, no doubt something lovely about the breeze from the open window, the curtains murmuring before falling still.

You don't mean to say you intend to sleep in here together?

Oscar's face was still. Constance could see now that the moistness in his eyes was not grief or not grief alone but was combined with terror, & in the company of his mother was further combined with helplessness.

You, darling, are a nocturnal animal. & Constance has... A woman needs her privacy.

Had this been spoken to another by another Constance would not have believed it. But believe it she did.

LJW didn't join them for lunch.

To the Avondale then, with the atmosphere cool & clear as if after a thunderstorm. Oscar's response to the interference from his mother—someone who would have told the Pope that he had his hat on wrong—was to become an ogre or a clown.

There was grouse & champagne. Grouse & brandy. Champagne & brandy. & lunch mere soakage for much post-lunch drinking.

Oscar when he drank turned himself into a living caricature. Constance assumed herself to be looking at a portrait in burnished oils of a bloated Napoleon surveying a battlefield: rarely satisfied & always on the hunt for a psychological abundance he could never find.

Later at the lodgings he was BOILED IN THE FACE yet saw his way to pick off many more brick-coloured glasses of the brandy which had stolen & hidden the good humour of the morning. He had adopted the soft & supercilious tone he was supposed to reserve for public appearances.

He may as well have been there BY HIMSELF. She certainly wasn't there anymore, yet on & on she would listen & laugh—the cackling was certainly taking it too far—until she began to pity herself for it.

He was TRANSFIXED by the brick-brown liquid, as if he had just been informed of a mix-up: the vial containing the magic elixir was filled with sepia-coloured poison & he was preparing for the agony of death slow & sure.

Why not? he said.

Why? she could have said, for by now he looked lonely & sad & baffled, the bafflement seeming to predict old age.*

Oscar excused himself to go to the bathroom, whereupon there was heard a sudden crash about which nothing would be said.

When it came time for bed, instead of anything more intimate he closed his eyes with the resignation of a man who wanted to share what couldn't be shared.

---

* Why is it, when you are faced with something you find distasteful, you insist on comparing it to something else?

Constance's knowledge of the havoc mothers could wreak gave her the licence to sum up their day.

Your mother is a suitably important figure in our lives. But we don't have to act upon her every suggestion.

Oscar might have been already asleep. Asleep he was not an impressive specimen of a man. Awake he had forgotten that they were supposed to be lovers. & how was she supposed to remind him in the way of a lover that this was the case? But weren't kindly reminders the dues of the sexual life?

He awoke with a shock in need of some water.

She feigned sleep, letting him rouse himself & sip from the decanter of wine she had left for him.

Once they had moved into the house, sex would be no more than a constitutional thing, if fear & discomfort could be said to be good for the constitution.

As if from her slumbers, she said, I do very much appreciate how respectful you've been of my privacy.

You're most welcome, darling.

He was gulping wine. She let him get some more down before continuing.

Almost to a fault. & no matter what your mother says, I don't want my privacy. & I don't like being told what to do.

I won't be in Paris, he said. I'll be in the next room. In order to worship you, I must occasionally do it from afar.

This is a strange way of going about it.

They kissed. But he stank, truly. There was such a whiff of shit off him that Constance had to ask him to pay another visit to the bathroom. In that interlude she imagined that the

Oscar of yesterday, the husband of yesterday, had died & a new one had unanticipatedly sprung to life. Suitably widowed & herself reborn, she felt they could resume kissing. He was mercifully compliant, although at first it felt like she was dragging him around the bed. But she began to sift around his middle & then everything got up & running.

Yesterday, she said. What was your mother insinuating?

Mothers insinuate, he said. It's their role.

Do you want for us to be separated?

Are we not here now?

Do you mean to say our honeymoon has been consigned to memory?

There isn't a bit of it I don't remember.

You don't have to explain yourself, darling, not to me. But what I mean to say is, if at some point I am to conceive & indeed you are to be the parent of a little girl, we will have to do a little more than we are currently doing.

From her sifting around his lap, Oscar, some kind of wizard, grumbled before producing an erection that was so astonishing & unpleasant that Constance knew one thing—it was going to save them.

She felt suddenly veterinarian, one who had been asked to put an animal down. & from this they tried to improvise a proper sex. For there was only so much she could do for him. & she was almost grateful when Oscar had to excuse himself to vomit.

They slept for another good hour, & didn't speak for another hour after that.

They were not on honeymoon anymore, she thought not to mention. She assumed he knew that too.* They sat down to breakfast, trying to acknowledge what had not happened without speaking about it.

Oscar kept on talking about the shelf in the dining room, sounding as he did like a petty thief trying to distract a wary constable. But she was conscious of the hidden weight lovers lay upon each other & that she was putting on him. Even if they never made love again, they had accomplished it once, more than once, an accomplishment that led her back to her yoghurt.

Oscar resumed fascination in his kippers. When he saw that she had finished eating, he took her by the hand & led her back to the bedroom.

The shock of being back at the source of their worry transformed into a startled sort of industriousness, that of a maid who had just been informed of her mistress's imminent return but nothing had been done.

You'll have me thoroughly worn out, she said. Have you considered trying to find a happy medium between none at all & too much?

I might have.

You might have.

But marriage & romance are two very different things.

He started with his fishy hands to untangle her hair. & they

---

* We were that morning producing a child. This was the pervasive thought, my only thought.

managed it in the end. For who was to say that sex had to be intimate or even friendly?

iv

Oscar was clayed up. Hours spent in the boghouse. She had him on apples, which either he ate whole or sucked from them pips to spit on the carpet. & she was wasting her breath if she was going to get him to eat something greasy enough to get him going. Pheasant was a leaner meat than goose but goose didn't interest him as much. No wonder he was getting so cranky—while insisting he wasn't being—not to mention roly-poly.

Never was he more cheerful than after a gait-altering & tasty-smelling poo, resulting in a spell of lordly behaviour followed by an absence of a day & a night & gushing notes sent on Savoy notepaper.

& if that wasn't love what was?

She didn't mind admitting that everything was settling down RATHER NICELY. Oscar was chattiest in the late afternoons, when he would have shaken off the night & before he had set his sights on future excitements.

He was careful about his clothes, not only in what he would wear but in how it would be laundered & looked after. Only occasionally did he leave filthy underwear in a heap on the bathroom floor, which was no more than a sign his mind was occupied elsewhere, if not on higher things then not on picking up his drawers. Late in the afternoon he would take his bath, after which he would stand before her meekly au naturel & cherub-pink. In his naked state, he was no more or less delightful than Constance imagined herself to be, which was to say they were made for each other.

If something was missing, there was nothing that was actually wrong. If she had seen so much in Oscar of which there was no reason to be fond (the smoking & the disappearing), there was a great deal that was surprising enough to allow them to love & laugh & talk & be interested in each other.

That they were in their own way enduring, however gingerly, was first a surprise & then a comfort. & if there was one thing that allowed her to resume her old fantasy of being endlessly fascinated by the world, it was Oscar's preoccupation with being impressive to strangers, which left him off-guard with the ones he loved.

The most delicious fantasy of all was the one in which The Oscar Wilde was really very boring.

So it was that they had already reached the point in their marriage where small victories were worth celebrating. One day not long after the truncated tour of Tite Street, Constance received from LJW a gift. The instruction on the note was to unwrap it in the privacy of her bedroom & then to play with it to her heart's content.

The 'it' was a not entirely lifelike penis fashioned from ivory. LJW, so she wrote, had a fine collection of dildoes & was altogether quite dependent on the sensations provided by a ridged shaft.

Constance put it in a locked drawer. She was very particular about what did & didn't GO INTO HER. Nevertheless, the keeping—the permitting—of secrets gave her a certain energy. They were becoming all rather elemental & nuanced, which was why in a state of suppressed glee it took her a week of knowing that her body had changed before she considered sharing the news with anyone, let alone the very man who had made her pregnant.

& the unnecessary & delightful thought occurred to her that she mightn't tell him at all & would one day present herself in all her glory. Proudly & only half sarcastically WITH CHILD.

She had as per the doctor's advice hidden away a sample of her urine. Quite how anyone could tell from the contents of a murky vial she had no idea, yet with or without all the requisite orgasming, pregnant she was.

She began frequently to hum, following with her forefinger the line of the vein jumping in her neck. Was this the miracle that was being presented to her? She could not have said what it meant. At least the trembling she knew to be a sign, for it was true that she was about to sail the high seas in a wicker basket.

How long would it stay? For someone who could hardly remember a week ago, forever was a very long time & would take some planning. & how could she consider the ludicrousness of the miracle when she feared that pregnancy would be not at all a gentle & blessed state?

Thoughts of fragrant nurseries were no comfort. There was

a small, still animal inside her. Her innards blear of weariness & lovelessness.

& lo, one dark & slimy day the tarpaulin taste of sickness arrived. About which there was nothing the doctor could do. The prescribed peppermint tea was about as useful as Oscar in a brawl.

There was little to do but be still. Since the child was begat on a mattress, Constance saw fit to spend most of her time on one. Idleness, & wariness of oneself, being the newest of the virtues. Indeed there were mornings when she felt cheered by the change in her & unwilling to resist it, & other mornings when it was necessary to ignore it altogether. & there were mornings when the urge to strangle Oscar overcame all but the LAST SLUDGE OF REPULSION.

There were days on which the only way to converse with him was through the door. She had been growing fond of carried bathroom sounds. But now with the door locked again & him behind it, she thought she could hardly not say why she needed in. She was resting her forehead against the panel of the door, momentarily soothed by the sound of splashing from within.

Surely you're clean by now, darling.

The cheery part of her assumed he would let her in.

You'll have to wait.

What are you doing?

Bath things.

& for how much longer?

This last bit was said through a retch.

She dared not encourage anything solid with any more talking. No matter how many times she tried the door it was still locked. At the edge of the bed, waiting to be kicked over, there was last night's bedpan. FULL. With the next few seconds in mind, she needed to postpone the nausea & ignore the bedpan & disallow their noxious combination.

The jerking was beyond her. & the bedroom window which so often she stood at to daydream was lying obligingly open. She peered out in an attempt to summon a plan of action before deciding, somewhat on the spur of the moment, to vomit into the street.

NOT TO WORRY.

Being sick had the affect of charging up morale, for it was another thing she wouldn't share with Oscar.

Whatever had turned her into such a haver of secrets, the exertion of it was almost as gruelling as the bad mornings. She would swallow them like food, for she had become very sure about having things of her own. & in Constance's case things of one's own consisted of the thrill in the unknown. A soldier under orders not to cough up secrets to the enemy.

It was not until he was out of the bath & half dressed before she took up her position at the door. If she was as stiff as a sentry, it was because she hadn't brushed her teeth after being sick.

What do you think of the decor upstairs in the new house? she said.

What about it?

I was wondering whether we should think again about how to do out the top-floor bedrooms.

You have my blessing to buy all the blue china between here &—the possibilities are endless.

When we move into the new house, what if we had someone to stay?

Mama wouldn't manage the stairs.

Aren't you supposed to be the clever one? she said.

Have we to worry about anything?

Not anymore, she said.

Rather than taking her own word for it, she told him then.

A child.

It had never occurred to her that Oscar would not at least act pleased. & yet, she was struggling to read him. He as the father was obliged to make some kind of remark, a gesture. Even with the windows wide open, there was hardly enough light in which to see him. The look he gave out was placid & cold, as though he were suddenly homesick.

In a moment of excitement—& anguish—she stood before him with arms waving.

Yes, darling.

Thoughts?

There are many.

You have not uttered one sensible word.

My heart must have overcome my mouth, he said.*

There was so much to say. In order to save them both from

* It's becoming increasingly pressing for me to interject, even though I believe the truth will be too much for you, as it is for me, & is a poor return for your patience & love. I was simply thinking of what to say. & what I should have said was—we could tell all the world to die.

a black depression something else would be required of her, the tact of a pallbearer.

Constance had to persuade herself that SHE WAS THE ONE in a daze. But hadn't she the advantage of prior knowledge? & had anyone forced them to have a child? Still less, no one would be forcing them to go through with it.

If we have a girl, Oscar said, she should foster feminine pursuits. Boys are partial to whatever it is they're partial to. Girls don't require looking after.

I can't believe there's a child inside of me.

I'm awfully glad there is. A clever, interesting, kind child.

Constance could only hope he was right, but she felt as though they were covering up for a shameful act. How could they not be proud of themselves for fulfilling the aims of a marriage?

She feared the bedpan was having an influence—good & bad—on the scene. She took it away herself & they lay on the carpet for an hour or more, succumbing to the silence she had feared would accompany the news. The mood was forcefully of confusion laced with devilment, just a suggestion of it.

You know what this calls for? Oscar said.

There was still the faint trace of vomit in her mouth. & more of it bubbling up.

As long as you don't say a celebration.

A small one.

I couldn't begin to see people when I'm feeling like cold soup.

As she felt Oscar's paws around her belly, Constance

decided that the best & most sensible thing to do was to be happy. She took the ball of his thumb into her mouth & bit into it, making a decision as she did so—to be happy, to have the discipline to be happy.

Is this a dream? she said.

Whatever resources that were stored up in their hearts were about to be drawn upon, or had already been exhausted & would not be replenished.

I should think not. Bite me again & I'll tell you.

She bit him again.

You've woken up, he said.

& almost at his instruction she decided then to fall asleep, to start all this over again & to wake up in the afternoon as a mother of one on the way.

But everything did settle down. & there was always the possibility that Oscar was worried. As it was she had misjudged him & the situation was no more sinister than this—he needed some time to get used to the idea of being a father. Over the following days, he went to great pains to be there & to be attentive, which she supposed could only mean that he was leading up to something: a celebration.

There seemed little reason why she shouldn't go along with it. But it was only then, with a gathering on the horizon, that Constance began for the first time to truly feel like something that had crawled out of a sewer.

Oscar, up early to be on his way out, crept into the bedroom with a cup of peppermint tea for her. It was another stone-coloured morning. Constance was wrapped in a bed sheet, &

he was wearing a bit much for a trip to a wine merchant if that's where he was going. The angora coat was immaculate & all wrong for such a menial task.

Of course, there were places he had to be, & he always said where he was going, even if she never listened. She feared that in the course of three weeks in Paris, with a little added Dieppe, they had gone from being strangers to being sick of one another.

Drink that, he said. For your heartburn.

Constance wouldn't be drinking any tea today.

What about the piles? she said.

Avoid sitting for too long. You've been at that window for over an hour.

Whenever I stand I feel nauseous.

Granted, she was still tired from not having slept the night before & was becoming accustomed to lack of sleep, to mornings listless & done for. Such cloudedness at this hour could mean only one thing: she would be flat out all day.

I won't be long, he said. & you have all day to get ready.

Or not ready.

The pong of her breath put a halt to his goodbye kiss as well as his farewell oration, neither of which she was in the mood for.

How in heaven's name shall I receive guests, let alone be entertaining?

No one ever expects that from you.

He was inching out of the room. If she could have caught him she would have suffocated him with a feather pillow.

It would be better, sometimes, if you didn't speak.

Oscar flung his coat onto the landing.

I shall send word that tonight is cancelled. In case we should have to issue our guests with helmets.

Constance gave the door another sideways glance, expecting him to disappear out of it. Her arms were trapped in the folds of the sheet & couldn't be raised to hug him, but she would have.

Think of the money we'll save if I'm housebound & invalided.

She could not put her finger on any one thing. It wasn't the house, nor the orders—the lilies that arrived almost on the hour.

Your mother was right, you know. One of us should get a job.

Don't look at me, Oscar said, kneeling by her side to rub her feet.

If he was so determined all of a sudden to be charming, he was going the right way about it.

Then again, wouldn't it be nice, he said, to go into somewhere of a morning & stay there all day? In return for which you receive a luscious stipend.

I never have so I wouldn't know.*

---

* I feel very lonely at the thought of having withheld things from you, but a week before this, I suppose not long after the day you told me you were pregnant, I had found myself to little avail in the picturesque surroundings of Chelsea School for Boys. The scene was beyond description, but let me try. The question of the day was—what could they do for a man such as

I fear that polite society has had its fill of me, he said.

& you of it?

We passed that milestone some time ago. All I seem capable of doing well is getting under your feet.

Oscar obliged her then by dipping down so that Constance could put her feet on his back. A human footstool, JUST WHAT SHE NEEDED.

Since you're so good at it, she said.

She had loved him from the beginning & still did. In the softness of his touch & in the patient way he set about the job was perhaps to be found a stripe of guilt. She was not going to confuse this with their worry for one another but she should

---

myself? Matters weren't helped by the fact that I've never been one for explaining myself. & it was quickly put to me that, if we were to proceed any further, I would have to do just that. I was there by recommendation. Did that mean I was to assume the gentleman was unaware of who I was? Believe me, I was not surprised to find out that the chap was quite aware of me—but not my work. My reputation would suggest I've achieved more. I am not foolish enough to suggest that I have no front, but actual confidence is in short supply. I told the man my reasons for seeking employment—that no child needs the anguish of an artist for a father & that I aimed from now on to do not what pleased me but what was for the good of the family. The chap was quite taken aback by my candour. Tell me, he said, in so many words, what interests you about being one of Her Majesty's Inspectors of Schools. I am afraid I'm a better judge of theatrical than educational types, & I had no good answer for him. What a bluffer I was. It seemed that their concern was whether pupils turned up regularly or not. I thought it best to clear up the fact that I had been a truant myself, & it did me no harm. To little avail. It came to it that I had to ask the man's advice. What was it they would have liked me to say? Believe me, if only they would have told me I would have said it.

have. & had she known this she might have been happier at the time.

v

The house was to be Oscar's finest hour, but there was still so much to do that they couldn't do & would have to be paid for. How they would afford to equip the nursery troubled her noon & night.

There was also the question of who they would have to live in & to look after things & from where they could be found & at what price, the chores they could get by with doing on their own or that Constance could do.

She preferred it when he was at home, & every now & again they were as giddy still as newlyweds. But they could not settle, & had never been able to, & Oscar was keeping up appearances ALL OVER TOWN.

Had he known, or perhaps he did, that as she was left each day in her room, determined not to make the best of what it had to offer, she was never more certain nor more hopeful that he was going to leave her.*

* While we're in the habit of confessing, the day before we moved house, I was sitting on a park bench engaged in my favourite pastime. Smoking & reading & being looked at. Enjoying the attention of passers-by, I finished my cigarette & flicked it into what I thought was an empty bush. These are, by the way, just stray thoughts from a weak man's rememberings. Gradually the park chatter was overtaken by a shout belonging to a handsome young man who approached me carrying the upturned cigarette. My missile

Such worries aside, she did not care what she did. & it was not so very different from life at the lodgings. & pregnancy offered relief, in that corsets were out. Once or twice she considered asking Mrs Nettleship to run something up, indeed a few messages were sent back & forth, but very soon her size & her mood—she was often furious at the smallest thing—were beyond any dressmaker. It seemed to be God's will that her body turn to a hard cake of lard. That was her calling. & the sage-coloured habit—for that's what the maternity gown was, something fit for a monk—came in fact AS A RELIEF.

For his part, Oscar appeared to regard her as someone or something holy. There was nothing else between them but the unborn child. He bowed his head & so on when he spoke. She would reply, not caring, to the top of his head.

She'd wave goodbye from the window of a morning, & when Oscar returned she would be where he had left her, still staring at the god of love moving in the glass. It was the

---

landed where it shouldn't have. & he might have been scarred. Scarred! I say. You know by now who this was. I had met Robbie before, about the place. Despite what they may have you believe, I am no worshipper at the Temple of Youth, so I disposed of the cigarette & bid him adieu. Must you go? he said. Having virtually thrown one at him, wasn't I going to offer him a cigarette? A stroll in the park of an afternoon wasn't going to do anyone any harm. Now I don't do much but wonder how he managed to tug at my heartstrings so. But I am known to be a soft touch. Indeed, it was on our stroll that Robbie took the opportunity to explain his predicament. His other problems could only be hinted at, but his immediate pickle was his mother's imminent departure for the wastes of Canada. If he was ever going to make it to Cambridge in one piece, he would have to endure enormous hardships.

swerves of emotion that were less predictable. There were days when she could do nothing about her life getting away from her. She could have mustered herself; she could have joined him for lunch or a visit to the library. But all day she would sit in righteous discomfort just in case he might return & see that she had managed without him.

Once the maid had gone home, & assuming Oscar was still out, too, in the evenings there was no one for her to talk to. The voices that came out of nowhere wouldn't go back there. Her insides bore the rapid blood. Her breathing was often pained & the burning sudden. His cheerful goodbyes—& their guarantee that he would at the very least return with flowers—were the worst part.

She would sit there & turn the words over or let them sit there in all their falsity. & she would be full of regret at the things she hadn't said in reply & wouldn't say, at her own falsity, the lengths she would go to to sit all day, pointlessly depriving herself of even a glass of water, & at the way she decided it was Oscar who had inflicted this on her when it was she who was piously to blame. Eventually she would drag herself to the kitchen to shout an oath at whatever Cook had left for her to eat, that she had refused earlier. But it was the first time in a long time that she had allowed herself breakfast foods for dinner. Who would have known that kippers were best eaten in bed? She would choke them down one after another until she was enraged enough to get out of bed & pace the room, entirely convinced she was the victim of a terrible tragedy.

By the time Oscar would get home, often deep into the night, or later as dawn was breaking, she would in a haze of exhaustion be ready to ask for a divorce. That he would never say he was aware of her turmoil only served to increase the fury.

What kind of beast would leave his wife to stew in her own grease all day & half the night? An animal in the zoo had more thought given to its welfare. She was not quite able to believe it. Between them they would share in an old-fashioned & uncomplicated screaming match, whose impetus would over the course of an hour have transformed itself into dull exhaustion & silence.

There were months of this. & then came the child.

Childbirth wasn't half painful enough to offset the let-down afterwards.

The baby—not much of a character from what she could tell—had a downturned mouth that wore a look of suspicion she could only suppose might change. Oscar, the meanie, called him a raspberry. There was a new name for every day, a new soft fruit. The poor little thing couldn't have known what was going on but was nonetheless needled. For all the faces they pulled at him, there came very little apart from blinking & turning pink in return.

She was not so much gloomy as bored silly. & she muddled through with the feeding—for there would be no wet nurses for the grandson of Lady Jane Wilde.

But the child was sympathetic enough when it came to latching on when he was supposed to, although it took a good deal of flopping around before Constance got the hang of it. She learned as soon as he drew breath to cry to stuff his mouth, & that for the first week or two was their entire story.*

Every morning they would peer into the cot, relieved & also impressed with the child, that he hadn't died in the night.

Were they bad parents, negligent? She often thought so. The nights alone brought with them a capacity for shame & aggression directed inwards & no sense that she could do anything right or not wrong.

Oscar's was a charmed life, as if he had been born into two families, one of them royal. When he would return from his revelling & later wake up to be presented with his son, a pillow of relief would envelop her—she had helped the child through another day that might have been his last.

& one morning, the child's expression appeared to change. He was hardly blinking; his eyes were shining & merry.

Is he judging us already?

He can hardly see you.

But any half-observant child would have noticed that Oscar was dressed to the nines & Constance was wearing a loose-flowing shirt & trousers. As soon as Oscar made for the door, the child, altogether alarmed, started to cry.

He doesn't want you to go.

---

* I don't mean to suggest that my feelings are of greater importance than yours, but more than I wanted to be alive I wanted to be a father to a little girl.

I assure you that's not the reason.

What is it then?

He's hungry, my darling.

Constance stared into the cot. For too long, her day's itinerary had been the child's to make. & were it not for Oscar, she would have felt no guilt at letting him cry. But the child was going a worser shade of russet than normal.

Dearie me, she said. Again?

The child was hungry at any hour, when he was supposed to be & when he wasn't. She thought of her own dinner, the liver that she hadn't wanted & now would have fought you for. The carpet too looked very inviting, & Constance would have lain down on it to sleep. Instead she settled him into her to feed.

The boy wouldn't fix to her breast & her milk was spilling everywhere but in his mouth.

If the child is hungry he should eat, Oscar said.

Thank you for that contribution, she said.

Only when the child's mouth magicked itself onto her nipple did she see herself on stage at the Wyndham Theatre, the baby in her lap suckling as an orchestra played *La Marseillaise* & the capacity crowd standing to applaud. For the child was unaware that it was impossible to simultaneously breathe & eat. Having drained all the milk & most of the fluid from her body, he was only slightly scarlet, which was just as well for he had been on his way to bursting into flames.

There was hardly the need for lullabies—at the end of

a meal, both son & mother would be close to bereft—but Constance, who was warming to the sound of her own voice, would sing one anyway.

In the dark blue sky you keep,
& often through my curtains peep,
For you never shut your eye
Till the sun is in the sky.

The birth had been at home, with Oscar present as a kind of watchman. At least he had had the good manners to look ashamed & hold her hand for so long that she had to shake it off. In the time it took for the baby's head to announce his arrival, a fraction of a second, she thought to obey the forces of will which would refuse the existence of any discomfort.

& she saw its face then.

A moment when she thought Oscar was being reduced to a fiery mush, & that he could do nothing to help her. She could see every part of him consumed by terror & a cold form of uselessness. She could not remember if she had cried out or if she had gone into herself.

But afterwards there was the pain, so much that she couldn't express it. She would never want anyone she loved to know how bad it felt. & then she was handed a small, purple, screaming thing & did what she was told.

Every night until the merciful arrival of Oscar or the nurse, whoever got in first, Constance & the child were cloistered in the nursery. Delicate fingers swirling, baby thoughts crowding into a frown. The crown bronze in colour & soft & real to the touch. The posture, arms up & legs splayed, Constance associated with something—& not someone—that had died.

But he was not dead, he was alive, & not in the way she had become accustomed to, for when he awoke he did nothing but look at her in the usual way with eyes wide open.

He smiled then the spookiest of smiles. It was not a murmur nor a cry, only a smile. & she could see his heart faintly palpitating. Only Constance could see it, only she was there. There were some wonders of the world with just a single witness. The nursery still had in it a plaster cast of Hermes of Olympia, & that was her wonder. She would not otherwise have believed a smile possible; there was no way it would have been.

Now that she had figured out how to keep him alive & that fact had been acknowledged, who knew what she could do for her boy? It was immediately clear that by looking out for this blob, formed & held together by bits of her & bits of Oscar, it was she who would be BORN AGAIN. There was very little that could explain it, that something alchemic was at work, a feeling of being cast together but with what she couldn't say. It wasn't something she could see.

Often had she got him up & fed him & all the rest, & nothing. Now, inevitably in the middle of one of her funks, he had recognised her. She had assumed he never would. She hadn't expected it to mean anything. The truth was that she had never expected him to stay. Every day she had invited a new reason why he wouldn't survive.

Oscar sometimes asked her what it was she wanted from life. & she had never answered the question, not truthfully.

What she had always wanted to say was: I want to be a mother. For she understood that she loved the child as much as something that was about to be taken from her. She had thought that Oscar would be the only constant, but not only was Cyril hers, he was helpless; she found that she could help him—with what? With her need for him. But it had taken the child to show an interest in her.

vi

There must have been various reasons why Oscar would have chosen to invite people back for another soirée in their drawing room. None of them were coming to her now. & did they have to make so much noise?

Listening to the silly song that had been sung on her honeymoon, Constance felt like she was hiding in someone else's attic & as though she had been sent up there in order to be punished. It wasn't that she didn't feel she deserved having been put to one side. She was such a bore with her indigestion. & there was as she listened a sense of inevitability. None of it, the disappearing—& when he was at home, THE HIDING—none of it bothered her as much as the insomnia he was using as an excuse for carousing at night & lying about all day.

She had rocked the child long enough for her arms to GO

NUMB. But the voices were coming through the floorboards & a tuneless wind was demanding entry through the window.

THE NIGHT'S BLACK TRICKS. The slender strands in her mind forming knots so small. Constance was fretful, feeble, idle as a tree trunk but less useful for sitting on. But sometimes when she stared long enough from the window, she felt in the night sky a presence akin to the fuzzies, & she connected this stirring in the air—the night moving—to the breath of love & she was tempted to think it was some kind of response from the Lord.*

As a wife & now a mother she had learned a few things; she had learned about Oscar's waywardness, his wayward tongue, & his appetite for spending all his time out of the home he had devoted so much time to. It was in a certain way the most delightful paradox of many so far.

To the child, she said, No, I don't like it very much either.

Eventually she raised herself & with the child in arms moved slowly towards the door, planning to do what she knew Oscar would have implored her not to—going downstairs & joining in. For she wanted to speak to someone who wasn't a pink balloon. She wanted a conversation with something that wasn't the top of a baby's head.

She could have shared with them all the events of her day, the day which had been an amazing adventure—for Constance & the child, that involved walking as far as the embankment of the river. Standing for a while by the railings.

* If only I had known I was competing with God.

HOME AGAIN, skirting the edge of Paradise Walk, where the stench was overpoweringly bacterial & raw & the urchins were more insistent than she was able for—the child was oblivious but she wasn't—& onwards towards home with a pair of them growling at her heels.

She had had nothing to offer a beggar & propelled herself & the child onwards, vowing not to return. The urchins, seeming to know their station in life, stopped bothering her the moment she stepped onto Tite Street.

That wouldn't work as much of a story, would it?

Away, away! My heart's on fire!

In order to shield the child from the smoke, she stood guard at the door.

Oscar & co. were having as much trouble noticing her presence as they were carrying the tune. But if nobody knew she was there, nobody would mind if she turned around & went upstairs again.

It wasn't shyness keeping her at the door—it was her house after all; she was paying for it. It was a case of being OUTCAST IN HER OWN HOME, a feeling with which she was quite familiar.

How annoying—Oscar had seen her.

She had been about to scoot back upstairs. It annoyed her further that rather than beckoning her through the smoke, he was on his way over.

What do you have to say for yourself?

Oscar put down the near-empty bottle he was holding.

Good God, I love champagne, he said.

Is there any of it left in France?

He started to make out that his friends had barged their way in. A young chap barely of drinking age whipped away the bottle from Oscar's feet & was disappointed to find it empty. But there would be more somewhere. There was always more.*

I was just saying to Robbie how impressive you were in labour. Such elegance in the face of—

To cut him off she said, Can any of those young fellows breastfeed? What about him? Does he fancy himself as a wet nurse?

Robbie would try anything once, Oscar said.

She had no idea who it was, but she knew his kind, in a way, since she had imagined his kind.** Oscar pecked her on the cheek, beckoning to this Robbie fellow & the others.

She would be glad to see the back of the entourage but the last thing she wanted was to be left alone.

We'll get out from under your feet.

That's not what I mean!

Oscar meanwhile was already down the stairs with the others at his heels. The close of the front door was the sound of total & utter finality.

That's wasn't what I meant at all. It really wasn't. Well, that wasn't your papa, off having fun. Just as we are.

---

* What more is there to say? I've learned nothing.

** Had those fears brought him into being? Perhaps Robbie existed before he existed.

She opened a window before sitting on the floor amid all the mess, which was hers ALONE to deal with.

The room was in chaos & at the same time desolate, without ANY TRACE OF A SOUND from anywhere—only the anarchy of empty bottles &, from outside, the city's breath & the rumour of the river hastening by, keeping itself at a tangent, as if like everything else in her life it was trying to get away from her.

She fanned the child's face but the lucky chap was making his own preparations for the day & was lost to the world.

Soon dawn would be upon them & that would be it.

He needed changing &, oh, how she was tempted to leave him be. She considered the temptation until morning. & the thought, containing its shameful dereliction of care, was as familiar to her as needing to go to the toilet herself. & her next thought, all the while throbbing in her head, was to leave him in the care of an orphanage. A life of his own without her in it.

Did this make her a bad person, any worse than she was already? Wouldn't he survive in one way or another? Wouldn't he? Wouldn't he in any eventuality find the life for which he was intended? Motherless & abandoned, who would he become? Who was he now? A suggestion towards a person.

For it was by now a case of him or her. & not only did she envy the child his sleep she begrudged him the smallness & fullness of his existence, the plane of freedom & total dependency upon which he floated. & yet wasn't this all because she had not had more than an hour of sleep in weeks—or was it months?—& in her was breeding a viciousness, a cold fire burning.

The child was wriggling. She urged him with all her powers to stay asleep, because a sleeping child in need of looking at was not the same as a screaming child. & when he did awake with the beginnings of a cry, a new day had begun, another one.

THE STRANGE THING was that she was learning to enjoy his smells. & wasn't there something soft about him? Perhaps it was the relief to be found in the moment between drifting off or rousing, the instant between sleeping & waking life when there was access to the briefest & brightest of ecstasies.

Don't look at me, she said. I mean it.

She rolled him around to hoist him up & off to the nursery for changing.

vii

The mess of the drawing room was nothing compared to the mess of the study. She was surprised at herself for snooping in there. But the child wouldn't eat—she was peckish herself—& needed entertaining.

The universe of good order they had been discussing for months prior had been draped in scarves & lit with lanterns. The room itself with its ceiling of gold was coming to resemble a brothel—& one suffering from neglect.

She was not a little surprised that Oscar hadn't produced much work in the time since the marriage. His intelligence & the accompanying weight of ambition was to be taken as a caution. She had by way of encouragement made herself stupid around him. & often when they had guests to tea, or they were out for it, she would notice that rather than addressing himself to her he spoke to the room in general. When he would ask her advice—on a new coat, always coats—he wouldn't take it.

She bid herself silent then.

Home was supposed to provide you with a sense of purpose. This hadn't been brought to his attention, & it wouldn't be, for Oscar had a way of avoiding the subject of money & work. He made a great show of taking meetings, which in itself was odd for he never discussed them afterwards.

She wasn't imagining it, but every interesting thing he said on the matter of writing amounted to NOT writing, did it not?

She was going to ask him this outright. He was one of the cleverest men alive & yet he had produced NOTHING of note.*

Carefully, for the child was wriggling about, she perched at the edge of the desk. It might have been better to leave him upstairs in his cot, but the idea to look through Oscar's notebooks had only just occurred to her & the urge was much too delicious to let pass.

The pages were many & the handwriting was that of a child struck down with some palsy.

He had been on about plays & articles for magazines but this was nothing they had discussed. Without further ado she laid the child on the ottoman & began to read on. She had read

* Not quite nothing, my love. That child in your arms.

a good many poems, but this was no poem—& Oscar was no poet.

There was no indication of who this piece was for or whence it had come. The story, which concerned a white rose being coloured red with the blood of a nightingale, seemed to concern itself with REJECTION & SADNESS. But she was further taken aback by the looseness & the sharpness of the words & the apparent ease with which they had been put on the page.

If he had been asked outright, he surely would have told her what he had been working on. Seeing such tenderness on the page was as eerie as having A GHOST READ YOUR MIND. This was why, in assumption of his embarrassment & her own, she would not mention what she had seen.

There was no avoiding the realm of trust & that by snooping in his private things she had betrayed his.* & she had been doubting him. Which was worse? Concealment, why? For the same reason as doubt, she supposed, which was this—let him have his secrets. So why not her? No, what mattered were their secrets &, lest they be destroyed by them, how well they be guarded. A secret couldn't be something you had forgotten. It wasn't a proper secret unless there was no relief from it & it called on you hourly.

It wasn't just the words. Or if it was the words they were accompanied by a mercy & grace which had been buried in

* Wasn't I supposed to be the secrets man? Dare I say it that you could have had some other weapon up your sleeve? Something sharper.

the carpet fibres & were floating upwards to tease & soothe her soul. She would, she decided, from this moment onwards ease off on everyone. & that included Oscar.

Sleep came down too deeply for amusing dreams, & Constance awoke with a start to the sound of footsteps on the stairs, her own exhaustion causing her fierce & disorienting irritation. The fondness she had felt for Oscar only an hour ago—what about it? Weren't love & annoyance becoming all the one feeling? & when she reached the door of the nursery, she was startled to see that Oscar, dressed in his smoky going-out clothes & tipsy, had the infant IN HIS ARMS.

Only through the armour of tiredness could she say, You'll be putting me out of a job.

Now one sees the use of having a night owl in the family, he said.

Some mornings he would be in so late as to miss breakfast. But she was aware that Oscar was smitten with his son. It wasn't something he was hiding, & the awareness of it allowed her to soften a little.

Is this what you expected, darling?

It's so much more than that.

Oscar didn't seem to heed his own words, for there was something else on his mind. Was it that once again he had given the night & the better part of himself to people he professed to have little time for?

Just one more thing, he said. I was thinking about a little sister for him?

That she lay down on the floor in mock-exhaustion did not mean she wasn't truly exhausted. The future felt suddenly enormous & in it she was resolutely & helplessly minute. She lay there in that fashion for a good minute before she was able to speak.

I'd rather recover from number one.

Do I take that as your answer to the question?

How do *you* feel?

Gender-wise in something of a rut. Mama would be enchanted by a granddaughter. What's to stop us, darling?

I could give you a few reasons.

It was painless enough the first time.

Morning was washing through the room, over them all. In a few minutes, Oscar—a man of all this renown casting a child's shadow—would be downstairs & sound asleep. But she was softened by the sight of him nuzzling the baby.

Oh, don't you listen to me. I'm a silly billy. Aren't I, Cyril? Aren't I?

Constance did all she could to avoid him over the course of the morning, but when he wanted to be Oscar was very persistent. There was, he said as he came to her bedroom, no time to waste.

He was as eager as she was taken aback. Occasionally he

had sought the healing of her lap. & she had never been one for shrinking from crossing the hall. But few glories had lately occurred, for seldom now did Oscar get the point. Starved of love, she had been left to her secret shudders. Each sound from his room a temptation to cross again & try again.

Oscar had continued drinking, & the way he kissed with his mouth open suggested he was teasing her. The words she might have said in response he would not have wanted to hear.

With the nanny upstairs & the child crying, she with great care attempted oral sex. When that became tiresome for him they went back to the garden variety, which was the last thing in the world she wanted to do. Her cunt was still injured & she felt it tearing further, & how much more gruesome this was than giving birth. She wanted Oscar to PULL OUT but there was no reaching him with words. Her helplessness—& his oblivion*—was enough to shame her & spur her on to the end.

They didn't afterwards talk as they normally did, not a word. She thought she was going to cry but it was NO DAY FOR ANY OF THAT & before either of them could think of something to say, Constance went to wash herself. In the

* Let me talk to you about oblivion. You will not say that I was so. You will not put that lie into my mouth. To ignore a lover's distress is to deny oneself to be touched by the hands of love. It amounts to a denial of all love. I wear no mask; I am as alert to the lessons found in the heart of pain as I am averse to any suffering in your body or mine. Suffering is no expression of love. Suffering is no expression of sorrow. Sorrow is not love. But love is sorrow. You, my darling, must learn to tell the difference.

silence that accompanied the running of her bath, she began to worry that she was AGAIN pregnant.*

viii

Having another child was not their first mistake, but it was the first one to which she admitted.

The firstborn was as unknowable as his father but a more meek & inward boy you could never have met. He was there, he existed, but anonymously, & they heard from him very little. He was so silent that often in the night she would again fear that she had died. & beneath it all part of her wished that he would.

What happened next?

The little one was born, & nothing about him, or her feelings for him, was regular. In his presence she felt powerful,

* At Henry Poole an amount of royal warrants lined the wall. Polished brass & many mirrors bestowed a heightened shine on Robbie being fitted for a suit. Suppose I wear this to the opening of your next play? he said. If that was the case, it would be hanging in my cupboard for some time. We were feinting, & sizing one another up. Aware of the risks of being overheard, & relishing the thrill. If Robbie was right in his thinking, I would in all likelihood become known as the finest writer in the land. He seemed to know better than I, although I was happy to accept his opinion as certainty. I don't mind admitting that I find flattery very soothing. & it gave rise to a musing: what if the Wildes were in the market for a lodger? This I whispered to Robbie, & his reply, that he was in the market for a new lover, was a thought that shouldn't have been spoken aloud. I was to say the least wrong-footed. He wasn't to make the mistake of forgetting that I was a husband, & that my domestic arrangements brought me no end of pleasure.

as though he had passed on to her some secret knowledge that was being spoken in a language only they understood—witness his gestures, the double-jointed finger-splaying of a show-off. Already his presence brought with it an eerie sense of resignation. This was one who was going to go his own way.

& how was it possible, compared to the other one, that she loved him so lavishly & so soon?

The pregnancy—another HALF A YEAR of dragging herself around—was everything she had feared. But the little one was something of a surprise package. His breathing would stop & then start. Waiting for Oscar to get back from his meetings, she would lay him out on the bed in the full light of morning, just to observe him blowing in & out.

He would do it then. He would hold his breath & she would hold hers. Having hardly had the time to introduce himself to the world, he was already performing tricks.

There had been days when she with absolute ferocity & certainty wished to strangle the bigger one in his cot, but the little one she urged through every intake of breath. While his brother was born midway through one of the gentlest of sleeps, this little angel out of heaven was so restless that despite having been informed that children didn't dream, she became convinced that he had been born in the middle of a nightmare.

Oscar took to coming into her room of a morning, not to see to her but to stand guard in the grey light, perhaps to chronicle his night terrors.

That was all they would see of him for the day. He was once sent off to register the little one's birth, & when he returned he could not for the life of him remember if he had even done so. If he slept it wasn't at night. If he loved the second boy she wouldn't have known. If he still loved her he seemed to have forgotten it himself.*

You couldn't just squirt out child after child in the hope that it would make you feel better about yourself. What were children *for*? To make the days so very long as well as fraught with danger. Constance the village constable, keeping the young men WELL & SAFE & ALIVE & every minute of it herself feeling closer to death.

Speaking of which, it was a night just before Christmas when Oscar came in smelling of outside. She asked him to hang his coat IN THE OTHER ROOM. He was, she supposed, as adrift as she was, for she had been paying note to the growth of his jowls.

Do you know, she said, I feel half normal this time?

It had become more important to lie. How could she say about the bigger one that he was always there somewhere in her heart, but her regard for him, she wasn't about to call it love, had always been less than she hoped it would be. The good days came about randomly & were DEVOID OF MEANING. Sometimes he amused her for an hour before she grew bored, & there were times undeniably when she could

* Here in this cell, you come to me at night. The spirit returns & is made welcome.

tolerate him all day, from which she would emerge exultant & quite confused.

She was familiar with SHAME, for it was her mother, it was her grandfather, Mister Death, & it was the bird on the Genoa windowsill. Oh, did she believe in God now. The worst of it was that He came to her only as fear. He came to her in darkness when He was to be expected to appear, but the residue could be felt all day & to the point where it was becoming impossible to distinguish between night & day, fear & love, God & fear, God & love. The passage from one to the other was more treacherous than picnicking on a high window ledge.

She saw no trace of fear in the children, but you could never be sure. The little one raised one arm then, like a champion. One month old & he was his own person.

Our little boy, she said to the cot.

Another one, said Oscar.

How would this have been different if he had been a girl?

I try not to dwell upon it so much that all I do is dwell upon it.

What do you propose we do with the boys we have? What do you propose we do? Please advise me so that I should do it.

It had been a busy season & probably Oscar's fatigue prevented him going any further. & she had used the last of the day's optimism on the children. Oscar's disappointment was ALL VERY WELL, for it made her wonder if they shouldn't have got a pair of terriers. Would he have turned a hair if she had exchanged one for the other? A child for a dog.

But did she understand that he was trying to say something that could not be said? Did they or did they not have two children for no reason? & would it have made a difference if this in advance they had known?*

If you stay pregnant forever we should have a better chance of parenting a little girl, he said. Indeed, if you stay pregnant forever, you shall never have to wear a corset again.

The reason for keeping watch over the boys was that she could not bear the change in HER OWN BODY. She looked no different, really—a bit broader, something of a bloat—but she had lost all interest in clothes, & in being a person Oscar might find alluring. Whenever she looked in a mirror she did so with an apologetic expression.

Oscar wasn't going out that night. She watched as with eyes closed & pacing between the cots he began to tell the children a story.

Who hath dared to wound thee? cried the Giant; tell me, that I may take my big sword & slay him. 'Nay!' answered the child; but these are the wounds of Love.

The softness of the words were at odds with the delivery. For Oscar resembled a lawyer giving a deposition; that was all she could think of—he was trying to send somebody off to jail.

He did perform well but children didn't appreciate a performance necessarily. & weren't these words familiar

---

* Did you not notice, or was it that you ignored, my eyes filling up? This would have been your chance. If you had never wanted any of this, you should have spoken up.

from her night spent snooping in his notebook? The sense of surprise she had felt on first reading them had not gone away, but the tenderness had.

A little over their heads, she said, but I like it.

She was unable to say that she felt once more confused & weak, & that she wanted nothing to do with her own children. But she hoped this would change, because it had to. She had stopped kissing the children goodnight, or in the morning.

You seem exhausted, darling, he said.

& you?

Before you say it, not from work. But I've been considering this quite revolutionary thought of yours, that there should be more money coming in than going out. & that it might be in our interests to consider a lodger.

A cry came out from one of the cots, startling them. This was not unusual, a child crying in a nursery, plus they were hungry; it was to be expected. But Oscar was looking to her to do something.

Perhaps you'll find us another nanny first, she said.

The door she had come through was looking very inviting.

Quite right. Do we really want someone to disturb our reverie?

Our wreckage.

Our paradise.

Our sanctuary.

This was a man who had perfected the abhorrent art of bluffing.

What is it you have to say to me, Oscar? Would you please say it?

As was her wont, she lay down on the floor. Oscar's expensive carpet was hard with dried-in vomit.

Don't spare the horses, she said.

He's been here already, although he's rather young for soirées.

As long as he's out of nappies. We have enough of them.

& rather full of himself.

You'll soon put him right.*

ix

COME ON IN, EVERYONE, make yourselves at home; that was the way of it. (But they were in need of funds & Robbie was a nice boy.) He & Oscar were already fond of long

* Robbie was not lodger material, was he? He wondered if guests enjoyed special status in our household. That remained to be seen. I had him believe that the garret on the top floor of 16 Tite Street was the envy of all of London. Had he known he'd be sleeping alone he'd have brought a teddy. I left him to go for the afternoon bath I liked to take while you & the governess were out with the children. I looked up from my reverie to find little Robbie standing there in an oversized robe. Mine. Did I startle you? he said, shedding the robe & most nonchalantly joining me in the bath. Now he had startled me. He seemed to be of the opinion that you knew to leave us well alone. I am physically larger yet Robbie was insistent. & he was threatening to drown himself unless I would make love with him. I got up & stepped out, spilling water everywhere, at which Robbie took a deep breath & submerged himself in my old bathwater. Even from under there he maintained eye contact.

conversations about nothing. & she couldn't help but take herself & the children out for walks.

At two in the afternoon, the winter sun was as dull as wool. So much mud underfoot & the houses on Paradise Walk were sinking into it. But she had to admit that as long as they weren't hers she enjoyed the sound children made playing

As for the boys, without having given consent for a walking tour of a slum, they thought it was great fun altogether.

One little urchin was staring & staring at them as if out of a photograph. Whether photography was evidence of her folly or of the presence of God she could never be certain. A deathbed smile, a child jumping over a stream: a photograph was proof it had happened. She had made the mistake of trying to catch speeding carriages & running children. She had been unable to capture the moon & was told often NOT TO BOTHER WITH THE SUN.

The pleasure came with the artful stain of light on the paper. The subject of a photograph took on the state of being forever open to the world while being sealed off from it. They heard & saw everything without answering back. One such photograph had troubled her, taken of Oscar in a new white suit—chubby & sweet, as if he wasn't looking even though he was. He was there in the picture as light & air & time, God lifting away layer after layer of being until nothing was left.

In photographs, existence didn't get close & hardly mattered. The articulation of his stance in those photographs, there was no question of its sincerity. An acid taste in her mouth as he would say the most silly things—the most evil things—& not remember them. For she could only marvel at what he was prepared to put himself through—heartbreak, running ahead of him always—in order to be better known.

Quite aware of himself, yes—but not half aware enough. What others thought of as aloofness she knew was terror. & she knew from herself the rumour & truth of terror, she knew about insects in the blood, how they move & double back on themselves, & she could sense the moment—pull the string, done!—at which Oscar would come & go from himself before the leaving. His blood high, his soul limp. The eyes on him black, pure black & alive, no little violence in them. & fear, too, of his own reflection & hers. For this was where their souls found each other, in disorder.

The street boy began scratching at her in the way of a curious monkey. She had to get through to him, for you could not mind a child without trying to get through to them. His hair was oily & luscious & she combed it as she would have done for any child.

His bones were sharp & he was not very heavy to lift, & light on her knee too. Once on her lap he settled a bit. She had worn heavier crinolines. But when she shifted him from one leg to the other, he nearly bolted into the sky. After the struggle to brush his hair, in itself a senseless act, she pulled his face towards her so that he could nestle himself in her neck for some of her warmth. Every part of him was pulsing.

The children were asleep in the pram. & when it came down to it, she was doing a strange thing; there was no rhyme or reason to it. Or there was reason to be found in his foreignness.

Why was the creature so in need of succour?* It occurred to her too late that the child was starving. Had he eaten all day? & was he was being STARVED OF LOVE? She wanted to take him home for a soapy bath & a pile of eggs & bacon.

Constance now gave thanks for all that she had: the prettiest house in London, the remaining people they paid to run after them, even the secret stories written by the children's father.

Coming up the road was a dirty-faced woman with two babes in arms. She was evidently something to do with the curious monkey boy. One of her babies was holding a package of beef bones & was attempting to suck through the paper.

Are you making soup with those? Constance said.

Entire families spent their days outdoors, & years of exposure to the elements had given the woman's skin the texture of old boots.

What are you doing near my children? she said.

Only sensible words made themselves available—the wrong ones for Constance to use in this situation.

You've misunderstood me, I fear.

---

* I feel more sorry for you than I am supposed to. I put myself at a disadvantage by saying so.

Oh, I don't think I have.
I have children of my own.
What you doing with mine then?

x

Home, home, home.

She unwrapped her outer layers while Oscar took the little one from his pram in order to hold him aloft.

Were you out? he said, for Robbie's benefit.

She didn't mind that he was being so much of a show-off, but neither of the boys liked being swung in the air.

Oscar! Be careful.

I'm always careful.

& to the child he said, Do one thing for me, won't you? Take after your mother.

Oscar was barefoot & his hair was wet—this was just as odd as his remark to the little one, even if she wasn't about to pass comment. She was more concerned about dinner & what would be Robbie's expectations of the catering. It had never occurred to them to cater for themselves, but they had had to cut down the cook's hours. & since Oscar was out most evenings, for dinner Constance usually had leftovers from lunch. At the beginning, it had been something of a treat. Only in the last few weeks had she grown tired of cold mutton.

They were, in the eyes of the populace at large, well off. &

they should have been at least that. But they weren't & Oscar had not known it before being told it.

They had had to let go one of the governesses & one of the maids, which had made a difference. Oscar of course had his doubts. He was in the most trivial of matters an exhibitionist, yet there was no one more conventional when it came to the domestic. She loved him for that.

Didn't she love him for that?

& so they had dinner the three of them, although it wasn't until the last minute, with the gravy congealing, that Robbie got at his place at the table. She assumed he had been told the time of dinner.

The dining room was as bright & cheerful as Oscar had asked for, yet the atmosphere was as muted as at Lancaster Gate. She was used to a little bit of talk with dinner. Sitting up very straight & with the cutlery heavy in her hand, she steeled herself to get through it.

Robbie set about eating as timidly as a hedgehog approaching a saucer of milk. He was really very young. Knowing it was one thing; seeing it was another. & he had on clothes that an old man would wear.

Eventually he said, Don't you talk during meals?

Constance was BEING QUIET; she was being quiet because she was imagining the exalted conversations Oscar & Robbie would have had under this same roof—while she was out on Paradise Walk—& she was quiet because Oscar had used to speak with her about his work but not anymore.

How could she say to the young man who was about to go

up to King's College that silence at the dinner table was one of her worst habits & that she abhorred it really & truly & she was embarrassed that between her & London's greatest wit they couldn't think of anything amusing to say.

Oscar's eyes were on the potatoes he was mashing emphatically with a fork.

You're not a farmer, darling.

He's a growing boy, Robbie said.

I suppose we do have healthy appetites around here, she said.

Robbie spoke to Oscar as if to a child. Are you going to eat all your dinner?

Oscar was wolfing into his food. That she had never heard anyone talk to him like this before meant she could only approve.

He seemed irritated that he had to chew. & she watched without any sense of judgement as he ate sauce off his knife. Was this something famous aesthetes ought not to do? Did he sup the gravy from his plate when he was dining at the Savoy? It was just one more thing he had learned from his mother.

That other MORE ANNOYING* Oscar was supposed to be

---

* That's the best I've heard. I bow. But I can do even better. I don't feel too compromised by saying that no one likes a show-off. I never knew why people expected me to but they did. Now I cannot bear the fact that it has become the better part of me. I depend on it & how I resent that I depend on it.

long gone to the lecture circuit. & here he was back; she was as well off accepting it.

Aren't you going to answer? she said.

He's too busy eating, was Robbie's answer.

You should be flattered that someone takes an interest in you, Oscar. & chew your food.

Yes, chew your food.

xi

The presence of a lodger required her to refresh the flowers & have better things put on for dinner. It had to be done. They had dinner the day after & lunch the day after that. Robbie at every opportunity & with apparent glee saw fit to prey upon Oscar's frailties. It seemed to her, disapprove as she might, that she was being saved a lot of bother. & thus they carried on the three of them. It was a relief when Oscar took to showing Robbie the libraries & doubtless the clubs with a tender care akin to taking on a third child.

Having company also gave her time for more walks. But no bright idea to sing 'Twinkle Twinkle Little Star' to the pram's canopy. Constance alone was soothed by it & the being out. But she was glad not to run into anyone. For the people that worried most were always the ones to act cheerful around her. Even they would have been surprised at the weight a person could carry.

Did anyone suffer more anguish than Oscar? She could not

tell anyone that her one & only slept with other men—this was not news, so why would she share it?—any more than she could talk about how much it cost him. She had no sway, not even his mother had any sway, but too rarely did she consider the harm that may come to him. The lonely grave that would have his name on it. As long as, rather than concerning herself with people that she hardly knew & who didn't know her, & didn't want to know her, she could find a way to let Oscar be more of a returner than a goer. Wherever it was he went. As long as—without having to be trapped in one—they could behave as if theirs was an everyday marriage, with one dutiful & careful husband. As long as that's what Oscar was occasionally. & as long as that's what people thought he was.

It wasn't even Robbie that troubled her. She was not desperately-desperately concerned about them spending so much time together. As far as she knew, Oscar had kept to their deal: no women, & there was really no point in worrying any more. No point, was there, in trimming the lawn when the chimneys were falling in.

Did Oscar ever wonder about her? He certainly never asked her where she went on her walks & she never told him for fear of an exclamation about their safety. She imagined her reply—that she didn't care one way or another for her own safety but she would never do anything to put her boys in the way of danger.

& where was her little friend today?

London was nowadays a town in which you could go weeks without seeing anyone you knew. But she had been back &

back again & had seen her monkey boy often crouched by a wall by the embankment, gawping at mid-air like he had never before seen a living thing.

There was NO SPACE in her life for a new obsession, even a passing visit to Cloud Cuckoo Town, for she barely knew what to do with the balls of fat already under her command.

But she had allowed herself the fantasy—was that not what life was? A fantasy sparkling on the surface of the water.

There was of course a separateness to this boy & his kind. It was not that he had behaved that way with her, but she had no business toying with potential predators—since that was what he was, a wild creature. Wasn't it a good idea for the children to see what they were, in their essence, & what they might become, & to know that those you thought of as vicious & a threat were no more threatening than & probably just as delicious as a rice pudding?

From the corner of her eye she spied him walking along as if he owned the river & in his hand twirling something even though there was nothing there.

He was from a distance not noticeably an urchin.

She didn't feel sorry for him & that needn't have come into it, but Constance could not have foreseen how forcefully she would be moved by this sight of a shoeless boy playing, if not oblivious then unaware of her presence. It was the ardour of his expression, a child with an adult's worries & a man's charisma, & as he passed her with ne'er a look—was there half a smile?—she felt from him the magnetic pull of something like the river.

What a PERFECT LITTLE BOY. & did he know her? He didn't. The look he wore was fixed concentration, but on nothing & certainly not on her. A blue tit might have flown out of his head & she would have been less aghast.

Had anyone known what she was thinking, it would have been as if they'd seen her naked in the bath with the water only half covering her baby body. She was tempted to call out but that was the work of a barrow boy & was something she wouldn't do. She thought instead she would hurry home to do something useful like lunch. Robbie would be at the crammer, & a meal at home with her husband would be a small sign of normality.

While it was very lazy of her, she was already resigned to making sandwiches. Cook was sick & a sandwich was all Constance was up to. Instead of food a thought came to her violently then. The boy may have been about to jump in the river. & the thought unfolded quite quickly into a full-on drowning & the abject sight of a small corpse washed up somewhere down the Thames.

This was one of her sillier flights of fancy. It had to be stopped. Also: she was more gullible when she hadn't eaten.

She had to walk to the water's edge to make sure the boy wasn't floating there, & he wasn't. But when Constance got to the turn for Tite Street, her boy was there at the top of the Walk & seemed to be beckoning her to follow. But when she got the pram down from the kerb to follow him, one of the boys—probably the little one—awoke & THAT WAS THAT.

On the way home, she wondered what she could say of this

to Oscar. Inconsequential as it was, she would not be saying anything. It was the events of her life that embarrassed her more than anything. For Constance had an income but no living.

She had quite a few opinions on the matter, none of which she was going to share. She was of the opinion that as soon as you defined yourself by what you did as opposed to what you thought, you became a slave &—whether you were a seamstress or a jockey or the King of Belgium—whatever occupation you chose assumed the position of your master.

It was, as usual, a feat to get the pram over the front door. She fell into the hall with an almighty clatter but Oscar was nowhere. Nor was there anyone in his study; he had been in there working when she went out. The little one, who was unable to sleep under his own roof, had by now moved on to a wail.

Either the stairs were awfully steep or she was unaccountably tired in the middle of the day. & Oscar's door was closed.

She climbed the stairs to the attic to see Robbie's bedroom door ajar, her sixth sense informing her of what had come to pass. She had been waiting for this moment for as long as she had been married—or longer, since the sunny day on Park Street—& had been in this state so long that her sense of doubt had become such good company for her that she did not question it.

She descended the stairs & knocked on Oscar's door.

Could you help me with the children?

Just a minute.

Have you seen Robbie?

No.

She opened the door to see Oscar in bed &, squeezed into a tight spot beside him, Robbie squirming like an eel. Had she her wits about her, Constance might have pulled him off the bed. But she could not have told you what this would have achieved—the passing on of her shock perhaps. & to that she could have added: what do you think you look like, Oscar, beside that slip of a boy?

Robbie up & left, she thought he did, for she could not tell if he was there or not. & Oscar was stretched out like a dead man, a posture that said—I am having the last word.

How could she have been shocked? The scene, recognisable from her dreams, had nothing in it that she hadn't pictured. At least they were all at home, said the voice of reason. & wasn't home a place of safekeeping?

It was Constance who spoke first.

Well, well, well.

What distressed her the most was how CHEERFUL she sounded. The urge to be polite was so strong that she wanted to ask Oscar if he had been having a nice time.

His chest & cheeks as he was arranging the bed sheets were raspberry red. Constance experienced not anger but an emptiness, the pleasant helplessness of stretching for something—a balloon, say—that was out of reach & bouncing away of its own accord. What relief to be unable to grasp it.

She sensed a presence in the room then. She was the

presence. For Constance was contriving to see herself & her husband as if from outside, through the eyes of an observer or an intruder standing on their window ledge: a couple in a messy bedroom in the middle of the day.

From that point of view, the reasons for the undress & Oscar's disarray would be quite uncertain, as would his—Oscar's—bland expression, & the way he was beckoning the woman—her—to sit.

There was no animation, no obvious discord, but what could not be ignored was the man's distress & the flinch he gave every time she spoke.

Was he bed-bound & in need of help? The intruder would not have failed to notice that she was refusing to offer any. Perhaps the bed needed changing & she was on her way out? Or she was saying something harsh that he was having difficulty accepting?

Great PAIN was written on his face. The observer on the ledge could not have been certain but some kind of silence seemed to descend on the room. This was one way of looking at the picture. Only moments ago she had found Oscar in bed with a young man half his age. He hadn't denied it, for nothing could be denied. & even though he was naked before her she was finding a way to not come to her senses.

That went on & would go on, for she was listening to her husband cry.*

---

* Let me remind you. I've been here all along. & here I'll stay. Let me save you the trouble of wondering. But I urge you to speak freely. I urge you to continue to speak as if I can't hear you.

& if all this reality was beyond her, if disbelief was now smoothly replacing denial, so too the tight feeling in her chest, as if it were filling with HOT & COLD GRAVEL, was nothing to worry about; it would disappear, & leave her—there it is, look at it go!—& be gone upstairs to the attic with Robbie, or out the door & down the street to be met with the indifference of her strange, beloved street boy.

Something downstairs was requiring her attention. The children. Now everyone was crying.

xii

Ten in the morning & the day over. Another one she had seen NOTHING OF. Feeding had taken hours, with the sense that the children were unhappy with her. She sang to them without knowing why & sat them up in their chairs. The little one knew what to do—eat!—but wouldn't do it. She glanced at him to let him know, & when the good little boy did eat he came over all surprised, as though he had been deprived.

Before there was any notion of Oscar stirring or any sign of little Robbie, she set about making her own breakfast—watching the oats swirl in the milk, waiting for them to expand, setting the table when the porridge was ready, eating slowly & taking as much enjoyment in it as she could.

Energy would be required for the day & it was best to act as if there was lots for her to do. She got the children bundled up

& out of the house, walking from place to place. It was only by chance that she passed Powell's locksmiths, where she asked if they wouldn't mind visiting the Wildes at home. AS A MATTER OF URGENCY.

Mr Powell did not ask any questions, which gave her to think about Oscar's comings & goings. More thought should have been given to the deal they had made (no women!), but she didn't want to include herself in the exchange. & the allowance of more freedom would yet encourage Oscar to spend more time at home, although freedom was not something on which she placed any value. It was for that reason that she envied the children their blurry youth & their ignorance, for it was now safe to assume that PERFECT STRANGERS knew more about her husband's habits than she did.

A quick ramble along Paradise Walk—no sign—before returning home with Mr Powell following on her heels.

It was only right to tell Oscar what was going on. She asked the man to wait downstairs while she knocked on the bedroom door.

At first she thought he was inviting her in, but the sweep of his arm was to indicate that Oscar was the room's only occupant.

There's a locksmith downstairs, she said.

I see.

You need your privacy. We all do, as your mother did say.

She was so far very surprised by the directness of her phrasing.

I understand what you might have thought yesterday.

Oscar looked well rested & smelled of cigarettes & the breadiness of recently occupied bedclothes.

Please don't assume to know my thoughts, she said. & I thought we made a pact. I think I deserve to know the reason why you broke it.

Robbie is not a woman.

The answer was far too quick for her liking.

What a charade.

I tried, he said. Our family?

Did it feel like a lie when she snapped, I don't want to hear that word from you?

The children were real, & her love for them, what there was of it, was real as well. & they would all be okay. They would have to be.

& the silence afforded her a moment's thought.

Constance knew that the marriage would hold its value, for she often remembered the morning of the wedding, & the journey to the church with her grandfather, & she remembered walking into the church, & that she was supposed to have been overcome. But she felt not much different now than she did then. It was only her good faith that had been tested. For very often when she was alone, on mornings less fraught than this one, Constance took herself back to that carriage pulling away from Lancaster Gate. She could see how things had not gone right in her life; but in being away from there she had achieved so much, all that she had wanted to at the time.

Whatever Oscar was going to say, she was going to ignore.

This she had told herself in advance. If he was to try to hold her, she would PUSH HIM AWAY. The footsteps on the stairs indicated the locksmith had gotten impatient & was on his way up.

Oscar didn't seem to mind that he had an audience.

I want you to know, he said. That in every other regard you are the love of my life.

You may find the law is not as accommodating as I am.

Can you find it in your heart to forgive me?

She picked at his collar, putting it up & putting it back down. She must have done it A DOZEN TIMES. The turquoise pyjamas gave out against the drabness of the day. In their marriage they had always been able to contrive a moment of intimacy per day, not so much by contrivance than happenstance. It was here, as Oscar flattened his collar, that they appeared to switch places. For she was more worried for him than angry; she couldn't have been less interested in being angry.*

Stories abounded of the likes of Robbie being dragged by the hair into police cells & locked up & left there. Even if this was WRONG, she had the sense that in the part of their marriage that had just come to an end Oscar had been trying to protect her from any of this.

The idea that he would continue to do so pleased her enough to say, You look handsome today.

---

* You were not to blame.

Where's Papa?

i

Life was only as boring & as hard as it was supposed to be. With more help to be had with the children, there was nothing & everything for her to do. Marriage had made an idler of her. The days were not ENTIRELY EMPTY & like someone demented Constance filled her world with mannequins, wools & vegetable dyes. But work would occupy a person for only so many hours a day. A bison could be taught to make a dress.

The only thing she ever needed to know was where Oscar was & when he would be coming. Wasn't it absurd the amount of energy that was absorbed by waiting for someone who was never going to arrive? & the less she saw of him, the more she was inclined to pretend that neither were they married nor did he even exist.

He still wrote though—good Lord did The Oscar Wilde WRITE. When first he started to take off for the night, she thought it delightful that he sent flowers with a long note. Whose husband, when he would be gone for no more than an hour, would send all those flowers? It had been the notes she had liked best. Now it was the notes that she discarded.

It was tempting to think his writing was getting worse, but she would had to have read the notes in order to have said so.

Perhaps he was getting better. She would find out tonight. & there was at least some chance of seeing him at the theatre.

Where's Papa?

The bigger one had the six-year-old's penchant for asking annoying questions, but he too had GOOD REASON to miss his father. He was, though, forever asking.

Papa's still at the theatre, darling.

Off having fun without us again?

He's working, darling. It's his big night.

Stuffed drains & the scarceness of plumbers had been giving Oscar the perfect excuse to stay away from home. Until she could find somewhere plausible to send them, Constance & the children had made camp with friends nearby. Charitable, patient friends.

When can we go to the theatre?

When you're older.

When we're *older*, called the little one from his grandmother's arms.

That there was never any need for LJW to babysit—there was no end of help at the Mount Temples'—was a sure sign that her presence in Cheyne Walk could be relied upon. It was her custom to turn up just as Constance was due out, thus guaranteeing her the boys' undivided attention for an entire afternoon or evening.

She had already been there long enough for the bigger one's liking, but the little one could not get enough of his grandmother, in whom there was to be found a sympathetic ear & endless indulgence. He had begun the day by pretending there was something wrong with his ankle, which once LJW got wind of it developed into a profound & terminal lameness.

Now he was unable to walk unaided. He had been absorbed into LJW's bustle but, by the time Constance got home, was bound to be woven into her hair. But she was determined to say nothing, even when the little one began sucking his grandmother's thumb.

He says work is very tiring. That's why he has to sleep in a hotel.

Your poor father is exhausted, LJW said.

I'd like to write a play.

Perhaps it won't take *you* several years.

It had taken Constance half the day then five minutes to get ready, her face taking as long to arrange as her outfit. All for what? A night alone at the theatre.

Again & again Oscar had told her that his work was about their life & yet not at all about it. Thus she felt fiercely proprietorial about a play no one had seen & she had no wish to see & had considered avoiding. She would have been just as well staying home. A new loaf of bread & a pot of honey would have pleased her just as much. Or some nice scramblers that she hadn't had to make herself.

& the odd thing was, LJW wasn't joining her for the evening. She must have known something would go wrong.

A prance up & down the room for her approval then, to the words, You have something on you.

Constance had earlier noticed the stain on her blouse. LJW without so much as a 'may I?' used a gnarled knuckle to scrub at the dried-in custard.

Aren't you getting changed?

Constance, forever beset by doubts accompanied by a peculiar form of insolence, decided that tonight's answer would be no.

There was no time & the theatre would be cold & since she was unlikely to see Oscar in all the mêlée she could keep herself buttoned up until it was time to come home again. & if she did see him with her coat off, he would have to make do with her with the custard fouling up her shirt.

The sign of her coat was instruction for the bigger one to run to obstruct the door, dragging after him his brother. It was to the bigger one's credit that he never once approached being ruffled by the little one's protests, which were at headlong level & were as effective as they were sincere.

The little one's restlessness Constance put down to missing his father. The predictably unpredictable behaviour, like the habits of a newly acquired hamster, was becoming his trademark. She wanted to put him in her pocket & take him along for the evening, for it wouldn't be long before he found his way to the theatres on his own.

The bigger one on the other hand could have done with losing some of the officiousness. & that sleepy look of his.

Oscar was still in the habit of coming home, just not very often & only for long enough to play Big Bad Wolf with the boys. & it was always far too apparent that he would go in the end—as if he had never been, & he had never lived there.

During those scant hours, they still managed idle gossip on every last vicar & renter that had crossed Oscar's path. He filled her in on what seemed like very busy days, before drifting into a maunder about the arrangements for the boys' summer holidays. The poor fellows had been billeted in so many places that she sometimes forgot they were all of them supposed to live under the same roof.

When they had said all there was to say about the boys' bedrooms, they would bemoan the lot of the modern parent & yearn for the days when there was nothing for them to do but climb trees in the park. They wondered if the little one would hold on to his curls, or if like his papa he would go from curly to straight to curly again.

The carriage had arrived.

Once the boys had been encouraged to go & pester the driver, LJW looked Constance in the eye to drive home the question, How often do you see him?

Often enough.

How do you feel about him now?

The only approach open to her was matter-of-fact. Worse than I could have expected.

So kind of him to lay on transport.

Oh, he's nothing but *kind.*

The more the custard had dried into the fabric the sweeter it got. She should have sucked more of it up.

I should have changed, she said.

Yes you should have, LJW said. & another thing you should do—

She went to the door to check that the boys were still otherwise occupied.

He has lovers?

This was said as if LJW was in a devilish mood. The playfulness hardly mattered & had but one effect, to fling Constance into a state of emergency. In her mind were answers, scraps of answers, the ends of answers without beginnings, & her silence was being taken as confirmation of the fact that Oscar took lovers the way some men ordered coats. In fact, coats were more expensive & less likely to blackmail or inform the authorities.

Take one of your own, dear.

If Constance wasn't careful, she was going to be asked to step out with Oscar's brother or the cab driver.

LJW became excited by the subject.

Don't tell me you haven't considered it?

I haven't & that's all there is to it.

Oscar had as far as she was aware kept to their deal. The sanctity of his word, even after all that, meant a great deal to her. The deal was only important if both sides understood that the terms—no women—were not the terms at all; it was just what they agreed upon at the time. The embarrassment she felt now was the embarrassment of not having fully entered into the bargain in the first place.

LJW walked her to the door.* As soon as Constance thought of seeing Oscar, her anxieties doubled. Worse than when she was wearing a corset, Constance felt her insides folding & arranging themselves into order.

Did you know?

One's mother-in-law was not supposed to be a confidante. & the question, one that Constance had been holding inside year upon year, made LJW look perplexed & sad.

I'm sorry I couldn't say it to your face.

It wasn't really your place, was it?

But nothing will really change.

Won't it?

Marriages don't fail. The arrangements just change.

ii

Constance & her aunt Mary stepped from the carriage & without anyone in the foyer to greet them wormed their way through the crowd of young men, the hubbub just another sign that Oscar's career was definitely on the up.

The stalls were heaving but seats were found for them in a well-placed box. Somebody—a painter of some renown—had told her that a person, when they were widely celebrated,

* Trust Mama to make it seem as if she owned the place.

became known for being known alone. Superciliousness, utter & unapologetic, with a weary disposition, this was what people had come to expect of Oscar. The worst parts of him*, in other words.

Her chaperone for the evening had never made any attempt to hide her distaste for Oscar. & Constance was perfectly willing to shove this back down Mary's throat as well as privately worried that her aunt had had it all right in the first place.

With that going on on one side, & all the excitement coming from downstairs, Constance felt apart from it as well as immediately & definitely disconsolate. It took all she had to imagine the poise back into herself.

UPRIGHT MRS OSCAR.

Whenever she was addressed in that fashion she sensed sarcasm, an attitude evident in the faces gathered in the neighbouring boxes & in the surface urbanity of the publishers & impresarios & their honoured guests. There were a few unusual sights—some had their laps full of others, like dolls; all the young chaps carrying with them a bounce of talcum powder, with all its associations of babies & old men.

Sharing Oscar with others had been a central part of their marriage. But it was so much easier when she wasn't in the same room.

At least her aunt's presence served to dissolve the energy coming from below. But Oscar's disciples—hardly a

* I will speak in a tone you'll appreciate. I'm less appalled to hear these words than I am to consider what you say as a fault. It's my dullness & my fears that I worry about. & you, darling? What is the worst part of you?

buttonhole without a green flower—existed in defiance of the likes of Aunt Mary. Since everything about her husband's cohorts gave Constance to assume that nothing they did was accidental, she had then to assume the flowers were significant. There would be no profit in knowing why.

& wasn't all this what Oscar had been working towards? To perform to a large & varied audience, to PERFORM ALL THE TIME.

She was going to see him afterwards & congratulate him & kiss his lovely lips if she got the chance. For this was not a commonplace event; this was the culmination of his career so far. It was the culmination of everything.

She WOULDN'T DARE wish the play to be a dud; she knew that would be wrong.* From what she had read of it, the script hadn't inspired much confidence. She had told Oscar she loved every word, for that's what he expected to hear.

During the first act, she couldn't help notice the fellow playing Lord Darlington. It wasn't just his gait that was the image of Oscar's. The stuff leaving his mouth was as artful as it was artificial; phrase after phrase was plucked from their domestic repertoire.

From the moment I met you I loved you, loved you blindly, adoringly, madly! You did not know it then—you know it now!

The words were as easy to recognise as they were difficult to stomach. But it was not the words but the context that

* Wicked woman.

she objected to, for the memory was as clear & undisturbed as the diamond on her engagement ring & had its origins in the same room. Here in the mouth of a ham actor was her past. A moment as mysterious & private as a prayer was being dramatised for all comers. Not only that but the delivery rang entirely false.

& no one noticed, for how could anyone have known?

Aunt Mary had fallen asleep in any case.

Wasn't it as though someone had come up to Constance on the street & repeated—proclaimed—a rhyme belonging to one of the children & was proceeding to take ownership of it for themselves? If she were to claim the phrase as her property, for it had been given to her, what would that have achieved?

& the play was REALLY QUITE GOOD, although Constance had no time for Lady Windermere herself. Such a ditherer. & the ending left too much unresolved for her liking. Who knew what when?

Aunt Mary had to be nudged awake once it had finished.

Did I enjoy it?

Thoroughly.

The audience was in restless & boisterous humour. The applause was long & Oscar appeared before the curtain, dressed more flamboyantly than ever. To look at him, he was not at all taken aback by the din. There was something docile, even bovine, about him. & in his buttonhole was the metallic flower sported by all the showy young men.

Aunt Mary gasped at the wanton cigarette-smoking.

For shame.

Constance would have gathered herself to applaud. With all the noise, she was able to do no such thing. Had Oscar even seen her? She couldn't tell. He may not have, but he noticed everything, did he not? He would surely give himself away with a smile or a pause.

He appeared relaxed enough to have been spending the evening at home, sitting in a rocking chair, nursing one of the children.

She began politely to clap. But it wasn't her husband she was applauding. *Her* Oscar was occupied with getting used to the adulation he had always craved & had fully expected. He was regarding them all—she was one of a crowd—with a sort of forbearance that had the effect of making Constance for one clap all the harder. It made no difference that she was his wife & that for weeks they had not spent a night under the same roof. Constance came to the conclusion that she had not merely been spared, but that Oscar had been preparing her for this very evening, & this moment, which was playing out not for his benefit but for hers.

He spoke then & THE PLACE WENT MAD.

Oscar had this casual habit, although nothing he did was born from casual habit, of overemphasising certain phrases & mumbling others. He was just as offhand when people misheard the lines he had deliberately thrown off.

The mischief of his comment, something with a great many adjectives, threw the assembled critics into uproar. Her own disarray, she supposed, was due to the relief at the thing being a success & it being over, although once Constance had gotten used to the events of her own life being parroted by strangers, she would have sat through another hour—if only not to have had to go & speak with Oscar, for she wasn't sure whether to go back afterwards or not.

From the bar came shrill voices in several languages, the humus odours of excitable men & dead cigars.

All present were smart-seeming & chatty, watery the lot of them. No one noticed her thus no one budged. She could not compete with their god & did not want to.

Her nerves were as raw as mince. Every step was an adventure, a misadventure in which she was conscious of being appraised.

& he was going to let her stand there.

It was another addition to the list of things she might try as her own career: the art of being alone in busy rooms, not to mention the art of talking when the room had stopped listening & the skill of not noticing or not caring when they had.

Oscar was holding two glasses of champagne. The glasses were not the kind they had at home.

No attempt was made to introduce her to anyone, & what people Constance did recognise—there were more than enough old flames to be going on with—she had no wish to engage in conversation, least of all with any Robbies. Oscar's little friends whenever they had been entertained at Tite Street were all alike: surprised & delighted that he had a wife & just as fascinated that she should be so hospitable & accommodating to one & all.

& wasn't she as set in her ways, wasn't she as judgemental when it came to people in her house? But tonight was another matter. & the distinction was that she was not in her own house.

Oscar, in company, was behaving as if life were one long birthday party. The tone of his voice had gone up a few floors & evidently his appetites for wine & brandy & whatever else were those of a prisoner on furlough.

I've caught you in the midst of things, she said.

He had not been caught out in any way, but Oscar gave himself away easily. The hand he used to stroke her cheek held a matchbook & written on it was an address she didn't recognise.

I won't keep you.

You haven't told me what you thought of Lord Darlington.

No, I haven't.

It was only proper that she should have congratulated him on the success of the evening, but jealousy, of the unknown & of all these strange birds squawking, had its own part to play. She was allowing it to take hold.

The children were asking for you.

The look that passed between them contained no charge or dissent or warmth.

You should have brought them.

Should I? Why?*

She set down the glass he had given her & looked around

* You were quite right. I was being full of myself. I am full of myself.

for her aunt. They made a curt exit then, taking the back stairs, where a man on his way up saw fit to speak with them.

I fear when it comes to Oscar Wilde, not enough people get the joke.

She could not escape Oscar. IT COULD NOT BE DONE.

It's no joke, she said, Mr...?

Allow me to introduce myself. Arthur Humphreys. Hatchards.

& I'm—

I know who you are.

I'd care nothing of it if I were you.

When she got home, LJW & the little ones were still up but half asleep. She should have carted the children upstairs as they were, but Constance felt like coughing them all awake. The five-year-old was only pretending, in any case.

Did you see him? LJW said.

I saw him.

Anyone else?

I did have a conversation, in passing, with a gentleman from Hatchards.

How did you find that?

A little dull.

Precisely what you need, dear.

Constance was not about to say that she had been considering that very subject, which wasn't to suggest that she was about to take up with the first man to speak to her in a stairwell. But an affair of her own would be a useful exercise in that it would allow her to inhabit Oscar's own reality, the part that was invisible to her & which she was supposed to find distasteful. An affair on her part would be something quite different from Oscar's & easier to justify.

She was never going to publish or give lectures or spend nights away at the Albemarle. It wouldn't be about sex.* Perhaps, if she were to believe herself, it was that having lovers of her own would bring their lives—& her idea of how they might live—closer together.

From the moment I met you, I could tell you were attracted to, & repelled by, the limelight which was my son's destiny.

LJW was so very often off the mark, although never about her precious sons. For she would have stood in the face of their Lord & maker to maintain that Willie was a saint in the making. Nor the other son, although LJW would have perjured herself to describe the particular wonders others couldn't see—the powers of Oscar's will, his fastidiousness, his temperance; she would very companionably have told you about all of that.

The children were sorely in need of bed.

& only time would tell if the world would come to know of Oscar Wilde's tidy ways.

For all that Oscar's mother was insufferable, Constance

---

* Our sex was hardly about sex either. I'm afraid you'll react badly if I attempt to console you. For I cannot much predict what humour you will be in when you read these words. If you are in good form you will be more likely to discount the fact—let's get it over with—that I enjoy male skin, young & delicate. But I don't much like to thrash around. Fondling then luxurious peace. Afterwards I like nothing more than to be still.

could see that LJW was dealing with something else entirely & that it was best to let her GET ON WITH IT.

He is a delightful boy, but Oscar is—Should I have warned you off him? You were so generous & kind to take him on.

Take him *on*? I love him.

You've looked out for him long enough. You must look after yourself.

iii

She had been thinking that life was VERY LONG & her patience for it short. She could not & would not consider staying in London for one more minute. All summer was spent looking at sunsets—in Margate, in Worthing, in Babbacombe—& waiting for something significant to happen. She missed Oscar, she missed her husband, & had taken to assume that within his widely professed regard for family life was included love for his wife. That a marriage was to consist of secret & prolonged intimacy was only likely to cause suffocation. Thus in a quag without reason to justify it, or the means to escape it, she began to revel in seeing nobody & taking no comfort in the people she did see. For it was not company she lacked but the ability to understand when she was lonely.

The children would get farmed out before she crept around in mufti with her Kodak. But the occupation was no more uplifting than the marshes she had begun to photograph. The act of catching light on film was as dispiriting as anything else she had attempted. It was commissioning a portrait of your own humiliation.

She would sooner have stayed away from town. But there was the very odd reason to be around. This Mister Humphreys was as keen as mustard, so she had decided to deliver the manuscript they'd been discussing in person.

She could just hear the slight—devilish, of course—that Oscar might issue upon the publication of any old book of aphorisms, let alone his own.

Mister Humphreys' office at the publishers was the set-up of a man with cerebral concerns. It looked as though he was afraid to be near other people. When he addressed her his gaze was uncluttered. & her nerves disappeared as his seemed to intensify—she couldn't help but notice that his hands as he read the manuscript were shaking.

He spoke right to her then. & the forcefulness, she didn't feel it before it came.

If you promise that we can work closely together, I might consider publication.

I should be delighted, she said.

It's work of which your husband should be very proud.

His voice, the tone of it, was kindly but bracing, a concoction as refreshing as adding berries to a tumbler of gin.

How is he these days?

There was no answer to the question. Oscar was wherever Oscar was. The letters that had begun to say less & less were beginning to arrive with less frequency.

Do you see me merely as the wife of Oscar Wilde?

Humphreys stood & drew himself to his full height.

How wrong you are, he said. May I ask if you are free to walk out?

Indeed I am.

He paused to light up before saying, What are we waiting for?

She knew the answer to that question. She didn't have to like it.

As Constance saw it, the relations between men & women were as straightforward & baffling as they'd ever been, offering her very little that wasn't a dumbshow—no heaven-in-life, if that's what she had been after, none of the telepathy to be found between mother & child. Certainly it was a matter for the soul, & hers had been sighing its indifference.

Wasn't that the way to go through life, to imagine as if it wasn't even happening? & yet, as they took their leave of the office & walked along in a direction of this man's choosing, the damp Piccadilly around her faded away with the thought that she might have been having a nice time.

Having nothing much planned for the afternoon & even less in store for the evening she was more than happy to let Arthur do the talking, never mind that it amounted to something of a confession.

I should be thrown into a pit full of fire for even speaking with you in this way. With my marriage, it's a very complicated situation.

I'm not one bit afraid of complicated, she said.

It is tempting to think that Oscar has left us alone on purpose.

Be that as it may, we are alone.

Albeit on a busy street.

More's the pity.

With the day bearing down on them, she ducked her head under a light rain. At Arthur's insistence, they had been on their way for lunch, setting off without an umbrella between them. There was something rather reckless too about having no appetite for food but being unable to resist an invitation to lunch. For Constance was too accustomed to the largesse of Oscar's lunch habits to be fully in control of her own.

Thus was the confusion that Constance felt able to ignore, for she no longer had any idea what was going on & would go on, for the great imponderable, Oscar, would not be cast aside like bad weather. She had never been able to fathom him but she shouldn't have tried. But she had not & would not cherish desire for anyone but him.*

---

* You hear from me, but I don't hear from you. So I have spoken to you too much, & seen you too little. No explanation for my behaviour will do you justice. & the actions of which I thought so little, or not at all, are recoiling, & the repercussions are being felt. I know this, I feel them. But remember that I was not made for surrendering. But now I do, I surrender. For here I am bid to eavesdrop, on what, & for what purpose? To hear the news that you had a lover, my darling. If that had a tune, I'd sing it. When we meet, when that happens, we will say nothing of this. For it is a debt nobody can pay. But I picture you with another, following him into the darkened room, whereupon my soul takes its own death-leap, & the mire awaits me, more of it. Haggard light, in my cell, in my heart. You had a lover. Perhaps you have one now. I am well aware of what I should say to that, & what I am

There had been so many days when anything she did amounted to a wrong turn. But on this, the most exhausting of thoroughfares, she had arrived at another kind of junction.

Look at all those people. Away with them all.

Had they any idea, any idea at all, what it felt like to be a woman at the beginning or perhaps in the middle of an affair?

iv

They weren't much living at home anymore, only visiting Tite St enough to maintain it, & then hardly. She only went there to get the mail—one for her, one for Oscar. One for Oscar, one for Oscar, & so on.

He was staying at the Albemarle & would be there either until it lost its charm or there was an issue with his bill, whichever came first.

At the porter's first glance, it was as if she were there to clean up. Then she was told that ladies day was a Tuesday & that she should have known that.

---

permitted to say, but why would I say it? For nothing I have read in these pages has stirred me as much. Have I allowed myself to be lured into a trap of my own devising? Perhaps that was your intention, with all my coming & going, to see me fall into it, having forgotten it was there. I have expected the exception to be made on my behalf not anyone else's. You're confused, you say. Why don't I believe a word? We have been separated, but didn't love travel with us; didn't it accompany us everywhere? My freedom, the stars, & the thought of you. That's all I have to keep me going. I'll speak you into the air. & so it will be, this ballad.

I know when Tuesday is—I have something for my husband. Do you know where he is?

She was asked to stay where she was. & she was asked then to follow the porter upstairs. She had been to the Albemarle too much for her liking, with no wish to be back again so soon as a delivery boy.

The porter slipped into one of the rooms, careful to close the door behind him.

She was told, He asks that you give him five minutes to get dressed.

It was eleven in the morning. When finally he appeared at the door of his rooms, Oscar's whale-bloat took over the landing. The slack look on his face confirmed what she had feared, that there would be nothing of any consequence said today. That was just the beginning. One eye was shut with either inebriation or sleep. The mouth she kissed was slack as well.

Well, well, well, she said. That took five minutes?

But he seemed & probably was HAPPY TO SEE HER. Even though they were only down the road, every time he asked for the boys he did so with a kind of regret.

There was to be no invitation to come inside. Nor was she tempted to ask for one. She handed over the mail with a curtsy.

Whoever was in there with Oscar was intent on the serious business of opening & pouring champagne. He—she was to presume a he—was carrying on with the grace of a lumberjack.

SHE ENVIED OSCAR his appetites, which was to say that she admired them. If he liked something, he would ask for more. & if he wasn't given it he would take it. If you were drinking tea & Oscar had finished his & wanted more he would ask you for yours. There being none left would be a signal to call for more. He would, if you refused him once, turn puce with injury. But refusing Oscar twice, so long as you were emphatic about it, guaranteed you a friend for life.

He looked the letters over.

Is it number sixteen that we live at?

She looked past him into his chambers, at the unmade bed. Bottles & bedpans.

You left home for this?

Don't you have a paramour of your own, darling? Who by all accounts is perfectly sweet & friendly.

That Oscar made a repulsive sight was not to suggest he was any more ugly than she was. Was she not in her own way just as bad? The glower in her eyes was a reaction of—again—her own soul, which came to her now as cold, empty, hard & useless, tempered only by her willingness TO BE STUPID & her readiness not to drive a conversation but ride upon it.

If you would be so kind as not to mock me, she said.

It agitates me to think of you alone, he said. Are you very hurt by my absences? I can see that you are.

The fact is, she said, your nature has dealt you a hand which you are compelled to play.

A boy came up the stairs, surveying the scene on the landing before going back whence he came. & now you have your mail.

When Oscar called after the boy—who apparently was to come back later—she was compelled to silence him & to warn him off further bloat. But caution had overwhelmed her to the extent that she pulled herself up & said, If you continue the way you are going, I don't know what kind of fate will befall you. Do you hear what I am saying?

I am well acquainted with the laws of the land.

& are you acquainted, too, with a stripe of discretion? It's all that's required.

Even with the children, there was never any point in warnings.

Clean your teeth, for heaven's sake, she said.

It was impossible to say ANY SORT OF GOODBYE. & Oscar was far too smelly to consider another kiss. Yet he seemed disinclined to go inside. It was down to Constance to hold her breath & turn & go, closing her eyes to deny it all, the sole effect being to make her knock into the bannisters on her way down the stairs.

v

Being neglectful of children only made them WANT MORE. Sometimes she forgot that she had little people at all, let alone such needy ones. & weren't they seeing the world after all? Other parts of England anyway, for they had to have some sea air.

Worthing wasn't so far away, & wasn't it A TREAT for them to see their father away from the distractions of London?

& what about love? Get back to love. She could not get

away from love. For it happened today that Oscar was coming to take the boys out. When she told them Papa was coming for some fishing, the bigger one chuckled. But she didn't mind what they did anymore as long as they kept each other amused. In return for keeping the noise below a roar Oscar often fed them a steady stream of sugar. His advice to his sons for when they got older—never turn up your nose at the offer of sugar.

She was glad the boys were getting out, but her trepidation over seeing Arthur had conjured up a warm sludge of a morning for them all. She did her best to pack them off without sinking into it.

The first few outings had gone well. But Arthur was too well behaved by far, & his half spoonfuls of soup were to be taken as mockery of all Oscar's appetites. She was in awe nonetheless of his way of filling postcards with so many small & legible words, his evident terror of making a mistake. It wasn't that she placed much store in handwriting, or conversations about train timetables. But when she considered it, there was a lot to be said for careful & there was a lot to be said for reliable.

They spent much of the morning on the beach. Mocking gulls sailing around above, the blue of the sky audible even over her awkwardness on the shingle. Constance only had to brush her hand across her own thigh to feel she was in some way betraying Oscar. But giving herself over to another, & another's hands, would be no more tremendous & indeed no more trying than a visit to the doctor. For wasn't sex A MERE PROCEDURE? Might it rid her of an ache or two?

If only to get it over with, she toyed with the idea of kissing Arthur there on the beach. But if Constance was apprehensive he was more so. There was also the challenge of having something interesting to say, & she was glad that he had decided not to rise to it. That they were facing France allowed her to speak of it without slipping into reminiscing. But it was Arthur who brought up the subject of her honeymoon. She dreamed again of high spirits on a rainy afternoon &, admiring her own sense of detachment, she thought she might take that as inspiration.

But her plan that they should go home together for the afternoon was starting to seem ludicrous to them both.

We must be out of our minds.

I'm not in the least interested in being sane at the moment.

Are you quite sure Oscar won't be here?

I'm beginning to think that you'd like him to be. He's gone fishing with the children, but he will be back at some point. If we are to go home, then we shall have to be quick.

One thing I'm not known to be is a fast mover. Nor are corsets the kinds of things to come off in a hurry.

In their early days—with Oscar, this was—she was all for those aimless lines of enquiry that might lead to revelations that, then, she couldn't get enough of. Although Constance did find Arthur fascinating, up to a point, she had no wish to know or be known by someone new. The feeling on her skin was suggesting clotted cream.

Even now as they walked back home she was wondering how Oscar was getting on with the boys. DROPPING THEIR

NETS & PULLING THEM IN! She hoped he had prepared some excitement if they came away fishless. Little boys didn't do well with disappointment.

An entire life spent looking out of windows, always at the same thing, & now her lot was to observe herself with every step growing hesitant as she approached the front door of a house she didn't live in. The key struggled in the lock. But she had been going around all day under a film of sweat & she was grateful for the dark of the porch. Off came the boots. To fall in love with one was to fall out of love with another. Not that she had never been aware of falling out of love with Oscar. The love was affirmed & lived on even as she saw herself inching closer to Arthur, who was half in & half out of the house, hardly seeming to move as he managed to land a kiss on her mouth. In that moment, with his cheek cutting into hers like an itch, surprise edged into irritation. Sometimes she had felt the same thing happening with Oscar when most assuredly he was miming kisses.

A commotion was heard then from the path. The bigger one rushed in with, Papa is here! The little one came next & with ne'er a glance at Arthur was soon satisfied that a stranger in the house held for him no interest.

He ran to join his brother in the garden, where they said their father was promising to build a rabbit hutch. Constance would have asked them how on earth The Oscar Wilde planned to do that.

Arthur turned to her with, A penny for your thoughts.

Hang on to your money, she said.

Oscar came in the door, half drowned.

They had indeed been fishing, for he smelled of fish. Either that or he had been caught in a flood. But he was quick to tell anyone who would listen, & how Arthur was hanging on every last syllable, that he had been teaching the boys to swim.

I had to; I turned around & there was Vyvyan underwater. I say, but I've seen stiller eels. Before you ask, I was calm, I was relaxed, & that gave the boys all the assurance they needed. Arms & legs outstretched. I made myself into a star in the water. I can hardly float, but soon they were kicking their legs & blowing bubbles; it comes easily when you're young. Putting their heads underwater is another matter. I couldn't bring myself to do that. So we rather made a game of it.*

Does that mean the boys can swim?

Not quite, Oscar said. I'll leave the rest to you.

The morning's slog was showing on his face, but he was more amused to find that Constance had company. & wasn't it typical to have his superciliousness appear as hospitality?

Knowing everything & nothing of each other, Oscar & Arthur fumbled a handshake. Arthur, in his alarm at being caught more or less in a clinch, & for reasons too numerous to mention in apparent awe of Oscar, had backed into the porch altogether.

By all means don't stand on ceremony, Oscar said.

A hutch will take all evening to finish, Constance said.

Then we have all evening.

---

* All we were doing was having some fun.

Oscar offered to take Arthur's coat & when it was given over handed it straight on to Constance. Then there was the matter of her bare feet & how far she & Arthur might have been going to go.

Her cheeks turned red as she explained that Arthur had taken a house nearby with his family. They were all having identical summers. But Constance felt insignificant in the conversation that she found herself in charge of. Oscar was too much of a showman to express any misgivings, & she should not have been astonished to find him so interested in Arthur & so knowledgeable about Hatchards' work, calling to mind shared acquaintances & seeming to completely forget that someone there was publishing books of his.

I fear the day at sea was a washout, Oscar said, as they walked purposefully all the way through the house & onto the rear lawn, where he spent an age on the wildlife of the south coast.

What are birds for but to remind us that we are earthbound?

She wanted them all to be in a boat now, so that she could have clobbered him with an oar. Until Arthur offered to go & introduce himself to the boys, Oscar was growing ever more contrary. He was not in on the natural world at all. What was he doing going on about snails & slugs?

The children were unnaturally cautious around the visitor who had dropped to his knees with the rabbit prancing on his head. With every day that passed, the little one was the image of his father. Was that Arthur attempting to pinch his cheek? Oh dear, it was.

The rabbit soon made a run for it, followed by the little one & then the other. It looked as though they were going to bury it under a pile of lumber. Once she was happy her children were not about to slaughter an animal in front of a guest, Constance went to get some water so that everyone could quench their thirst. She had lost her appetite for anything else.

The drink just about choked her, but she pulled herself together to have a glass & pour another in the hope that Oscar lately had become interested in paving stones. For she could have no idea why Arthur had chosen to talk about the use of tar in street coverings. The distress in his voice, the aimlessness that she had come to think of as charming. There was nothing Constance could do to help the poor man. She was sorry to have brought him here. She wanted to go inside, or for Arthur to go away, but the air at last was as warm & lovely as a fresh pancake. Nor did Oscar seem as restless as he normally was. Fishing had been beyond the beyond, but there was never anything wrong with the boys spending the morning with their father.

Arthur drank his fill then excused himself to find the boys, with whom he was evidently fascinated. But Oscar wouldn't hear of it. He thought Arthur might like a sandwich & that Constance might make him one. There would be no sandwiches.

Oscar leaned back with his fingers laced behind his head, as if composing some tribute to the sun. She could not remember the last time they had reposed together in this way. Her thoughts on their love were so pell-mell & so strong that they were best not remarked upon in a summer garden. She tried instead to conjure the sound of bees—but made do with the garden scents, which ripened into the smells of Hyde Park.

Had she known on her walks what lay ahead of them, would they have gone ahead? Who could have believed that parenthood would be so brutal? It was, & she had felt so certain that it wouldn't be. Days ended without her knowing if she had caused the boys harm. Today had gone quite wrong. & she feared that by having them here she was causing them harm now.

The sweat on Oscar's brow, a drop of which was making its way down his cheek. She wanted to whack him over the head with a block of wood. This was all his doing, this awful day. Oh, there were the boys throwing themselves around, mud pies in the offing. But she begrudged them their innocence. She was considering telling them all their father had done. Was she that cruel? How she wished that they had returned with nets flapping with fish. It would leave them with such a lovely memory of their father, if ever he was to be gone from their lives.

Oscar must have been having the same thought for he slipped into a private reverie & some minutes passed rather awkwardly, until Arthur came over to say in a lowered voice that he really had to go to the bathroom.

He was acting as if permission was necessary. & with a rather formal gesture Oscar granted it.

Was it likely that she would never see Arthur again? It might have been that he had all along been an apparition. Indeed, there was no reason to believe that he had ever existed. With a sense of elation, she told herself that he never had.

Afternoons like this one took the life out of her. But once alone with Oscar, she could feel again the God of Love. Either it had been hiding in the long grass or the woods or it might have come from THAT NOISY SKY.

Have the boys eaten? she said.

Oscar glanced sideways with a look that could have been kind or cruel.*

Your feet look nice. I've always preferred you just as you are.

I'd like them to have something soon.

As you command.

For pity's sake, please let's do without that.

& what shall we have? Tea & toast?

I beg your pardon.

Used to be enough.

Useless to chide him any further, even though this was no time for the sort of teasing under which in the sudden absence of the God of Love she might suffocate.

---

* If not for the hungover boatman, who fancied getting drunk again, I would not have been here to witness any of this. I am in no doubt that this Arthur meant very little to you but comfort, for comfort is the reason we exist—comfort before love—& you had to find it somewhere. & had I believed there was something in it, I would have left you & this fellow to it. I would have supplied the grapes.

There was no wind to liven up the ragged garden. She looked around for a dandelion head to pluck at. She fancied running rampage with a lawnmower.

Don't pity me.

I don't.

I can sense you being—I thought you were only a fool in public.

Are you still mine? he said suddenly. However it was meant, it came out like more of a boast than a query.

She looked up at the sky then, for she had lately taken to looking directly at the sun so that she might disappear into it or that it might blind her to the utter hopelessness of things. But it was not blindness she was seeking at all but silence.

There had nearly been a lover. There was her husband, whose own lovers were never far from her mind. One of them might have arrived at any moment. As if the more the merrier. Or rather, the pitiless thought that she was among the number of his lovers still. It was a comfort to think that she wasn't.

As long as she was alive & he was alive, their love was if not the best love certainly enough to survive on. Give her someone—lover, adversary, or foe—to take his place. One of the children perhaps. Yes, there was no question. Those two had supplanted their father in her affections.

The garden was a lemon haze, unforgivable then to think of the boys vanishing into it like sprites. Wouldn't it have been an act of kindness—perhaps it was her duty?—to let them trot off out of the garden to another life in which their parents were still together & still very much in love?

Oscar was waiting for a reply to his question. It went against all her heart to say, I think it would be better if you stayed away.

Those words, in her voice, were revolting. She smiled & waved to the boys as she caught sight of them preparing a bonfire. Burn the blessed rabbit if that's what you want to do. Or, if it would please everyone, Arthur would probably have offered himself to be sacrificed.

Tell me, Oscar said. How boring is he exactly?

Merciful heavens, I've just had an hour-long dissertation on the iron hand printing press.

Then why are you in such a hurry to be rid of me?

She allowed him to take her hand.

May I add, she said, I have seen no evidence of a rabbit hutch anywhere.

That must explain why the children are so happy to see me.

All you've done is build their hopes up.

What Did You Say, Darling?

i

First light. A stripe of sweet orange against the sky. TOGETHER they are watching a stray cat dander along the windowsill. It is not the cat but the little boy's head, as small & neat as a cauliflower, that she envies. Yet when his head rests next to hers or under hers it gives off a hum, the kind of energy that once confused Constance & caused her agitation.

This is the calmest she can be without being asleep. & sometimes she wishes she could sleep forever. For it isn't just LJW who has gone; the breath of love has been leaving them too.

Oscar will die at the news. & as he leads she will follow, for there is the likelihood that she will feel closer to him in death, & already has leaned too much on the habits of grief. Grief is a game—whose would be the most significant?—&, as in all the best games, there is something valuable to lose. Mister Death, no gambling man he, has it so that the person dying suffers less than the ones left behind.

Her illness is not nothing. She often thinks of herself about to die, even knowing that all the doctors proclaim her to be perfectly all right; but the last few months have foretold a state that is not worse & not better than a slow death, for she is simply dying, & whenever she lifts one of the boys up to her, if the little one would only go back to sleep in her lap, it is his vitality that she feeds on & takes for her own.

It is not that she wants to choke the little one. But the stray is off & he wants to see where it is going. There is no reason for her to prevent him looking but she will have to set off for London later & she wants to hold on to the morning for as long as she can.

The little one is grunting. He says he's GOING TO BE SICK. She would have been better off letting him go.

She takes a seat at the dining table, with some small solace to be found in the impassive sea. Robbie must think so too & that it is the done thing to block someone else's view. & she cannot remember the last time the sea offered any uncomplicated pleasure. There is as much to be had from watching rain soak into a dirt path.

She was the love of his life, she says.

Robbie is about to offer some consoling words. She won't let him.

She was!

You've never let him down, he says.* You're a credit to him.

I'm still not agreeing to an annuity, if that's what you're

* I have a strong feeling that his comment doesn't make sense to you. The thought is an alien one.

getting at. I can find it in my heart to forgive anything. Disingenuousness is another matter.

She smiles, very sweetly. The matter is closed.

The little one comes back in with an armful of fruit for breakfast. & he has yanked off some viburnum for his dear mama. What a good boy. In throwing himself into her lap, the oranges go everywhere & Robbie, ever the obedient servant, runs to gather them up.

Since you are full of good intentions, she says. What do you suggest we do about telling Oscar?

Not a peep out of the visitor. Isn't it down to the woman always to find not only the why but the wherefore?

The little one heaves himself out of her lap, the chair scraping off the tiles covering up her gasp, which is involuntary & quite sharp.

I alone ought to know how much he needs a mother.

Could Oscar not have run away somewhere warm & been imprisoned there? If he were in Naples she would have left already. Some soft words in a fragrant garden, sliding past all that with news of the children & how well they are doing in Italian & in general. This being the Continent, they might allow her entry with a bag of Turkish delight or nougat. An English prison is another matter. For when does one think of Reading prison & nougat in the same sentence?*

If there is a way to enter London without a word, DO THE BUSINESS & RUN, that's what she would do. Announcing

* Oh, for a life in which a sweet tooth is considered a worry.

herself would be to risk a brouhaha. If she were to bump into anyone, she might say that she's back to see Mrs Nettleship over a Continental wardrobe. The excuses come very readily to mind.

& she has had a right to wonder what kind of reception she might receive, for word has reached her of the gossip & that she is one of its primary subjects. Once she became aware of the talk, the thought of it was enough. Achieving the status of curiosity—becoming another Obaysch the hippo—has very little going for it, even less so now than then. Perhaps she deserves the sticks & stones & perhaps she can count herself lucky to be able to recognise the fact? Isn't that THE VERY OPPOSITE OF SHAME?

Does that mean that you shall go to London?

I do believe that's what should happen.

One of his friends can do it.

He can't hear this from anyone else.

The viburnum, she could cut some from the garden. But would it last the days by train & boat & train? Perhaps Oscar wouldn't be in the mood for flowers, & who is to say that he deserves them? Aren't such wild & lavish things better left where they are?

ii

The porter has a good handful for himself. Useless even in Italian to say it would serve him to remember that she is someone's wife. Robbie having noticed this, & the fact that Constance needed the porter's help to board a train in the first place, says, You could think twice about this.

Not my forte, she says. Thinking twice.

I count it as a privilege that we are making this journey together.

Yes, Robbie.

How long do you intend to stay in London?

As long as it takes to get permission to see him.

What if they won't let you in?

They will.

May I warn you, Reading prison is not—does not make for a very uplifting day out.

You must think me very delicate.

The days of being separated from the boys are gone. & their little faces as all the bags were being fetched downstairs. Constance pulled the little one towards her. As usual he had on him an amount of oranges just waiting to tumble everywhere.

She took one.

Dear heart, I will make sure Papa gets this.

Just the one, he said.

Robbie is still talking, something about Oscar's bankruptcy. Usually she can reply without thinking about it. & she could very well be missing something important. No, he's offering to take her hand, which is very nice of him. But his hands are pale as cream & as damp, & his suit is crumpled. In this carriage light the linen is very drab.

There is plenty she could be saying to the like of Robbie, plenty. But she doesn't want him to know how she is feeling, that they are about to travel through France, & France is where she & Oscar spent their honeymoon. Presumably it is there he will flee to once all this prison business is out of the way. The beautiful day has none of the brightness of the first morning at the Hôtel Wagram; the Mediterranean sky is vast but is guarding itself & its secrets.

Constance has no such defences. One faraway morning on honeymoon, after they had been taking each other's measure, she found the young porter dozy & bereft-looking in the hallway. Oscar was away buying books. What could she do but speak to the boy? Perhaps sometime he might bring with him a brush & some tooth powder & she would assist him in the needful. Here she was on honeymoon, fated to the brushing of a strange child's teeth. This was not her duty but nor did it seem to be anyone else's.

He turned up the next day & followed her as instructed to the bathroom, where he kneeled before her as if to be blindfolded & executed. The thought did cross her mind, for the child's hands were trembling & he was taking unnecessarily deep breaths. She cupped his face to shush the whimpering. A pinch on the back of the arm got him to stay still. Careful then not to retch as she tilted the head backwards—with nary a notion of whether he knew what she was doing, or why, or if she was doing it properly. A bad gas (she hoped it wasn't poisonous; it might have been) flowed from the boy's mouth into hers. But his beauty—about which there would be no talking to Oscar—was just as amazing as the smell, & when he looked up at her he could have been looking deep inside her. She is sure now that she loved him for that.

Barrelling towards Nice-Ville, the train follows a coast indistinguishable from the one she lives on. She remembers those occasions when the past meant nothing & the future everything & she almost laughs out loud, for now the reverse is the case & there is nothing she wants to do about it.

A picture forms of Oscar at the villa of a morning, feet up, having already been out with the boys. They would have found what they could of the fallen fruit &, if there wasn't enough,* would pick more in anticipation of the day's plan. Later in the day, when it would be too hot to go outside, she likes to think they would all of them together start in on some marmalade. They could get Francesca to do it, but Oscar has been apart enough from the children & wants to see them as much as he can. & later, when the marmalade is on & the children would be excited enough from all the sugar to have disappeared into the garden, she & Oscar would be left alone. There would be a necessary sense of resignation, the acknowledgement of troubles shared & the worries which have taken all this time to fade.

That is not all, for she hears talking too.

& the words are easy to conjure, for it is THE WORD OF GOD she hears. You are not alone. She hears it as surely as she hears the wheels of the train pass along the rails. The voice,

* There is never enough.

so unlike anything she hears in daily life, says coolly that the children will be looked after.

But she does not know who is speaking at all, & what does it matter, for Oscar is with great dedication stirring the marmalade pot—look at all they have made!—& cutting the orange peel into fangs for the boys to play with. What they have made is more than enough for breakfast the next morning. Oscar asks about staying the night in her room. There is silence then, from God & from Oscar. If something else needs to be said, SHE WILL BE THE ONE TO SAY IT.

The scenes are of course heavens-made.

With or without good reason, the fuzzies have returned. & by the time they roll into the station, Constance, despite feeling like she has travelled down the Zambezi under an eiderdown, is breathing love.

Sensing Robbie's curiosity, with passport in hand she leans forward to whisper, I fear I'm committing a criminal act by undertaking this journey.

Oh?

I'm still travelling as Mrs Constance Wilde.

iii

The horse pulling the cab is agitated. May she recommend a move to the Continent? For isn't London so vague in a mist? & smells of MISTER DEATH &/or things dying unnaturally. A city ignored by love & progress.

She has forgotten how to behave here & what to do, that you must be short with people & expect the same in return. It did the same to Oscar in reverse. How wearing it was to pick their way along the street; if there wasn't a hand to be shook there would be one expecting a coin. & you would always have to be careful of yourself.

She doesn't remember saying goodbye to Robbie but she must have done. Did she at any point mention to him the pain she was in? She had preferred to dig her nails into her palm, for she had read, & this was backed up by the doctors various, that to sublimate your physical self was A FORM OF GRACE.

But not a gorge did they pass over without Constance wanting to throw herself in it. & passing through Paris then, for a desultory night in a hotel Oscar would have sniffed at, all the while a feeling coming over her, that she recognises now. For she can see the turn for Lancaster Gate, & she changes posture but not outwardly. A young woman, with an upturned chin, her eyes open as a sunny day. She sees herself on a dark landing or at the bedroom window leaning out. The silence presses against her, forcing upon her more silence. To enter that door & climb those stairs—the floorboards shining, the carpets breathing—will be to return to a world before Oscar & the time before she had drawn the full breath of love.

She cannot see it; she cannot even picture it. & now that it is gone, more & more she has found herself on the point of sleep thinking of Tite Street. This is so that she may dream of it. Sometimes she sees in the rooms a soirée or one of the usual gatherings, & perhaps she is alone with the children. That is how she remembers it, from this vantage point, however much it pains her to see a ghost walking those halls, quite desperate to come to life but unable to.

Isn't it a relief that her powers of observation have waned? So much easier to be eloquent about small boys & orange groves. Travelling through all of France & enough of Italy for her to despair of leaving it had involved sitting & sitting & thinking & thinking overly much.

One dark day like this one she sat in a carriage with Oscar, nervous hand in nervous hand. Often were they on trains & often were they silent. He had taken off his coat & she was wearing it in her lap. The day had hardly gotten light at all & the streets were empty.

Had they been cleared for the occasion?

She spoke to say, What is it?

You tell me.

Don't you know? Can't you tell?

I can tell, yes. But I'd like you to say it.

Should I keep it?

Finally, Oscar replied, something suitably sad & important to say that she should do as she pleased but that he would like very much to have his way about another child. But not enough to say what that was.

The memory does not send her down a dark path. For the little one, now, is as ROBUST & FASCINATING as an acorn.

She sings to herself an Italian song, a love song, & comforts herself with the thought that she has forgotten how to be a soloist's accompaniment. & the status she has lost she never truly possessed & had never wanted.

The Oscar Wilde is gone, good riddance. But she wants so much to see Oscar, to see him first of all, &—no matter how tired & no matter how pale—to whisper in his ear & bathe his feet & take him home to clean sheets. The bed made just right, the sheets not too tight. Clean sheets always got him going.

The fuzzies are back, are they not?

& tomorrow they will be alone or near enough alone. She pictures the room in which they will meet. The walls, the wardens, the noises off. It is not the reunion she would have chosen & that is one reason to be hopeful. For neither she nor Oscar chose this, LJW did.

But Constance will not allow that woman to have the last word. Whoever else happens to be there tomorrow, it will be just the two of them. & though she does not expect to feel desire or even tenderness, other better feelings will have come to take their place. What she has not considered before now—oh, there is a lot she hasn't thought of & she can hardly begin now.

As long as the day is not wasted. They will only have so much time. At this stage in their lives, a morning together is not to be squandered. &, as she always has, Constance will take what she is given & will be grateful. She has never learned how not to be.

iv

The picture from the carriage—London dark as night, & impossible to distinguish sky from mist from mud. She feels the wind in her ears.

In Marylebone, she is not prepared to see someone she knows—oh, what's she called? It's Mrs Nettleship, of course it is, walking even faster than she normally does, as if everyone knows full well where Constance is off to & is there any need to announce the fact?

Isn't it a relief not to have to call out, for they are making good time without any interruptions & is there really any need for Constance to see anyone at this time of the morning? There is all the time in the world for other people. Aren't there a hundred dresses she could order & have made?

There have been more letters & gifts of books from Arthur. Later in the week she will agree to some visits; she'll fill up on the lunches where she'll report to everyone on all things Oscar & the way his circumstances seem to suit him. A measure of privacy & some proper time to think is all he needs to make his masterpiece.

At the gates, a guard without a word goes through the few bits & pieces she has with her: tooth powder, photographs of the children, & Vyvyan's orange.

Name?

Mrs Constance Holland—Wilde.

Visiting?

Oscar.

Oscar who?

She enlightens the man with the picture of the boys.

The sons of Oscar Wilde. Delightful, aren't they?

The orange, for the heinous crime of coming by train & boat from Italy, gets confiscated.

I need that, she says. Do you hear me? I need that.

What is the likelihood of the fellow sneaking the orange for himself? Another guard takes her away to a room watched over by a strange & kind warden whose face has subsided in a way that suggests savagery by a dog. Not much has been left behind & he can barely move his mouth to speak. Constance must assume she is to wait where she is.

She thinks of nothing as she waits. She knows better than to think too much. She will only end up with the feeling this was ALL HER FAULT.

There is in any case nothing to say other than the prison is as welcoming as the inside of a bell. But the warden goes about his business in a way that she decides is related to care rather than watchfulness. He seems in fact to be virtually on the point of tears when he produces the keys to lock her in.

She starts to talk then, asking the man about Oscar, his well-being & spirits—an amount of questioning which in everyday life would appear rude. But Constance expects no answer & she is happy to have no answer, for she doesn't know what is going to happen to Oscar after all this & she doesn't suppose he knows.

As for the warden reciprocating any of her curiosity, it is to the door & perfect silence that she asks if they could find it in their hearts to provide tea.

Evidently you aren't supposed to ask for anything to drink.

She has a stale bun on her; she might eat that. No, they took the bun at the gate, didn't they? She tries again more forcefully & the warden returns with a mug of tea, stewed & lukewarm.

In this bell-light the tea is blood red. & before she knows it she feels quite at home, saying to herself that the order of events has been ordained. &, since this is all the work of the Lord, she has been chosen. Into the mug she blows the breath of love, but the tea—or the Lord—doesn't do what it is supposed to.

She had it in mind that a cup of something would soothe her, but it holds her attention at least, directing her thoughts inwards & elsewhere, which at the moment the tea takes effect is where she feels she is, dazed & tired, but happy to be back in the company of her two boys, reminding her of the man she will today leave behind her in Reading prison, who left her behind all that time ago, which, in the likely & cruel way these things come back on you, was his loss, his entirely, for he has missed out on so many treasures, the grace of small boys at breakfast, before the day has gone wrong on them, the little one & his oranges of course, but the bigger one has become much more proper, just watch him—he never once glances up from the task of slicing the loaf, spreading butter all the way to the corners of the bread, all the while saying nothing & giving nothing away other than a ferocious anxiety that this be the most carefully buttered bread in history & that she should feel privileged to be a witness, but she is more than that, she is his mother & it's not difficult to say why this moves her so now, today of all days, for there is no mistaking who the bigger one takes after, & whether this will be borne out later in life she doesn't know but she hopes so, & hope is important, for it's a long time since she dared hope for anything, especially on behalf of the little one, who has enough to be going on with & who will do just fine whether his mother—or father, for that matter—sticks her nose into his way of going about things, which is not only the best way but the only way & he won't change for you or for anyone, an outlook in such a small child which is to be envied, but more than anything it is to be admired, for he is so like his father yet so like himself, which is not as half as maddening as it sounds, especially on mornings where she has to say goodbye & leave him in the care of strange & unreliable governesses who at the very least help him make the most of his Italian lessons, but Constance of all the people who should mind doesn't mind if her little fellow wanders to the window for a look-see or to wave a white handkerchief, if only to amuse himself & probably the others, too, in a way that only little ones can, with the sincerity coursing through them with a velocity that would exhaust a strongman, & even the thought, that he is her entire life, occupies her with such a strange force that has Constance catching her breath while being grateful for the capacity to still breathe at all & for the quiet of the cooling tea which she draws into her greedily so that she might pass another moment without blubbing & covering the day with more shame.

She looks up to find the warden waiting for her. She hands him the cup, but he doesn't want it.

Before you go inside, he says, may we ask one favour? There are two little boys on his landing. Petty thieves. Naughty boys, nothing more.

On her way quickly to the door, & Oscar, Constance says, What would you like me to do about it?

He asks if you could see if you could manage to pay their fine. Perhaps they could be on their way?

At the end of the corridor a door opens & she steps through it, glad of the fact that Oscar has someone to keep him company.

She is led then down a dark passage leading to ANOTHER COLD ROOM—a jail within the jail—where she finds her darling trapped behind cold bars. He is absorbed in the task of tearing a coil of rope into single strands.

He doesn't seem unhappy, he really doesn't. Gingerly she takes her seat without him appearing to notice.

The actor playing her husband is dirty & thin. She can't imagine he's constipated anymore. On his face is an expression she recognises. Constance was always so surprised in private by Oscar's piety—most of the time it came over as hopelessness—& there it is now. He is as soft as a novice nun.*

* Recently expelled from the warmth of the cloister.

She can't touch him; she can't even reach him. As if holding his hand would bring him back to life. It would be worth a try.

Oh dear, darling. Are you all right? You're not, are you?

Everything is weak. Even his neck hangs loose. Those lips of his look burst & the skin on his cheeks is red from burns or perhaps it is broken from all the drinking. Even though he has had to give everything up, the hard way, she wonders if it will repair. It probably won't. Would she have guessed it in Park Street or in that busy hall in Piccadilly that their love would end up here? If she had guessed it she would have been glad to settle for it.

& there is the smell of fresh spew.

It's just too much to think of him hanging over a bucket. It is best not discussed. She can imagine him having those discussions with the wardens; let him have them. Wrinkling her nose does nothing to stifle the smell or to make him aware of her presence. But she is grateful for this pause, for no one tells you what to say in a prison or what not to say. Oscar is not a bad person. In the eyes of the law he behaved wrongly, & for one so clever he was certainly a bit dim to bring all this upon himself.

Who in the world gets it right all the time?

& to look at him she hopes, out of pity & for the sake of explaining it to herself, that there is more bad behaviour in him yet. She would help him out on that front—it isn't the worst idea, in the circumstances—although neither of them seem fit for anything very piquant.

They were lovers; they weren't always here. & they were better at it than they thought they were.

& isn't she as haggard as he & without prison to blame?

The warden is watching. Well, well, well, she says to nothing.

Hasn't Oscar been a decent father? Better in ways than she is a mother. It is as well that she has for the time being some say in the matter of where & how the boys will see their father. But wherever he goes when he gets out, rather than them being in his, she wants him to participate in their lives. That's the correct order.

Visiting time is running out, isn't it? She can't stay here all day.

I'm trying hard to think that you're all right. You are all right, aren't you?

There is time yet; the children aren't going anywhere. Even though there are things she knows that Oscar doesn't. Somebody here is sick & it's not him. What would he say if he knew? What would she say?

When all is said, what is there left but pain?

He's in enough pain. She saw that in him too late. & what use would she have been? She could have wished it gone & shown him what in return? More of the fieriness that he craved, her busy mind, & at the centre of it all her dullness to match his.*

* Shall I tell you what was on my mind? Brick walls painted a blinding white, pipes, buckets, a peephole. The night before, I begged the warden for some bread, however badly baked. When he said, Breakfast comes in the morning,

I've been getting your letters, she says brightly. You're still better on the page than in person.

Oscar shakes his head then. Is he not up to talking, or not up to being teased?

Have you been brushing your teeth? she asks.

Having debated whether or not to carry the picture in a frame—she prefers not; not is flimsier & CLOSER TO LIFE—with both hands she holds up the photograph of the boys.

They haven't forgotten you.

She knew it would not have mattered what she said about the children. Just the mention of them is too much.

Of course they haven't, she says. I brought you one of Vyvyan's favourite oranges.

I know.

Oh?

I can smell it on you.

But they took it off me.

I can smell it.

Regardless?

Yes.

She lifts her hand.

The boys have gone mad for foreign fruit. I did try them on the celery—it's not like any celery we have ever tasted—but

---

mate, I told him I could never face a morsel before noon. At least that raised a laugh, & together we stood at my cell door to watch from across the landing two young boys being dragged along in handcuffs. Mere boys, what crime could they ever have committed against humanity? I asked. Stealing rabbits, came the answer. I could only hope someone was looking after them.

their eyes are on stalks every time they see an orange. The little one especially.

Is it that LJW dying is a footnote to talk of the children? THE VERY EXISTENCE OF MISTER DEATH is an aside to life, by which, safe in the thought that young life converts all & makes it beautiful, she means her boys. At the root of it is the worry that her own life has all of it been in vain. A marriage of love, true in her case & over before it began.

I dream of them, he says. & you.

Come along, Constance says without rancour. You don't dream of me.

& my mother. I dream I'm in her house & you have come to tea, which I've made, not too badly for once. Everyone has taken their leave & only we three remain.

She would like to propose another dream, in which she is serving tea, steeped as they liked it, to Oscar & his mother. A fragrance like that day's biscuits is in the air & LJW is in convulsions; Constance is unsure of why. As the bellowing grows deeper & deeper, Constance starts to list the reasons why mother & son should be left alone. With breaths of love it is they who will make the ascent to heaven. At the very moment the reason for the laughter becomes clear—Oscar has burned his mouth on the scalded tea, that is all—she comes to the conclusion that there is no room for her in this picture. She sees Oscar, FAT ON MOTHER'S MILK & running after rabbits, playing Horsey or Big Bad Wolf.

Mother & son alone at last. & later the evidence accrues. Before going out of an evening he is building a fire & in a small boy's voice Oscar is fussing over what to do & his mother is telling him where everything is supposed to go & Constance is struck by how difficult it is to be true & how you can't please someone who REFUSES TO BE PLEASED & is no longer there to watch.

Oscar is staring at the air as though diamonds are suspended in it. He is talking about those days in Park Street & he is raising his voice now to talk about his day with the boys in Worthing & how it would be to live again as a family.

The wind goes out of him then.

You're appalled by the prospect, I'm sure.

Families don't get appalled, she says.

If only she could remember more of that day she might understand why a reunion would be a good idea & how it would work for him as well as her. For it is not something she has seriously considered, nor is it something she wants, not now & not soon. If there was any true way to go along with it, she would.

She ignores him, & if that isn't love what is?

She has come to say what she has to say. The one woman who can save him is gone. & how strange in the life of a painful marriage to have no one to turn to apart from the source & host of the pain. A son & a mother are the full expression of intimacy & its limit. For that's what it has come down to. & this moment.

I love you, she says, following it quickly with, & you love me. But I came to tell you something about your dear mama, that she died.

Oscar sits up as straight as he can. But the remembering & talking has taken all his strength.

LJW was not much of a mother, not by Constance's reckoning. But he was her son, yes, & without the completeness of his mother's faith, & the most cack-handed of adoration, would he have ever written a word? He might instead have lived the pleasant life of a clerk or a teacher. A mercy that would have spared them all.

Did you understand me, darling? She loved you, the best love.*

To Constance Oscar softly says, What did you say, darling? & to the warden he asks, How long do we have to go?

Time, comes the answer.

She would like to take Oscar for a walk, but that is rather missing the point. She would like to put her face close to his so that she might with the breath of love properly say that when you marry you marry until you die & when you marry your one chance at love goes with you. Another life would grant another attempt at it but SHE HAS HAD HER CHANCE

---

* The little lost boy, that's what you're getting at. The visions roar but fade quickly, do they not? I have very little to tell you about the little lost useless boy, unreachable through these foot-thick walls & still less across the expanse of all he has done against you. I count my crumbs for you; the smoke goes up from my chimney nightly. Does it drift your way? Is it visible? Do you owe anything to it? But wit deserts me here. My love for the children never. One half regret & one half hope. Did I miss anything? The feeling is more than love, & will outlast the injury I have caused. For the law has decided that I am unfit to be with them, the universe has decided that I should never see my mother again, & you will decide, won't you, that I am not worth sticking with.

& will not marry again. & Oscar must know that he can take this for granted.

When she goes in the end, the breath of love may go with her or it may not. It may live on without her knowing it.

The guards know what they are doing; they come quickly to get him. Oscar with nothing to be ashamed of & with no one left to impress prepares in perfect silence to be taken away. Constance gathers her things,* discovering in herself a sudden optimism about the day & where she may go for lunch &/or dinner.

You'll be all right, she says. We all will. & we'll see you when you get out. Come for tea? We'll look after you.

Can that be done?

It can by us.

* When I saw you I wanted to turn myself in every direction but the one in which you were facing. When you left I almost went out of my mind, & I am going out of my mind now. You told me, didn't you, that everything would be all right, but you have your special way of letting me know that it won't be. For I have caused you so much pain & given the chance I would cause you more.

About the author

Andrew Meehan's fiction has been anthologised in *Town and Country: The Faber Book of New Irish Stories* and *Winter Papers*. His first novel, *One Star Awake*, was published in 2017. He lives in Glasgow.